Cum For Me *Volume 3*

Slippery When Wet

Lock Down Publications & Ca$h Whispers

Cum For Me 3

A Collection of Erotic Tales

•

Lock Down Publications
P.O. Box 1482
Pine Lake, Ga 30072-1482

Visit our website at
www.lockdownpublications.com

First Edition April 2017
Printed in the United States of America

This is a work of fiction. Names, characters, places, and incidents either are products of the author's imagination or are used fictitiously. Any similarity to actual events or locales or persons, living or dead, is entirely coincidental.

Cover design and layout by: Dynasty's Cover Me
Book interior design by: Shawn Walker
Edited by: Mia Rucker

Stay Connected with Us!

Text **LOCKDOWN** to 22828 to stay up-to-date with new releases, sneak peaks, contests and more…

Thank you!

Submission Guideline.

Submit the first three chapters of your completed manuscript to ldpsubmissions@gmail.com, subject line: Your book's title. The manuscript must be in a .doc file and sent as an attachment. Document should be in Times New Roman, double spaced and in size 12 font. Also, provide your synopsis and full contact information. If sending multiple submissions, they must each be in a separate email.

Have a story but no way to send it electronically? You can still submit to LDP/Ca$h Presents. Send in the first three chapters, written or typed, of your completed manuscript to:

LDP: Submissions Dept
Po Box 1482
Pine Lake, Ga 30072

DO NOT send original manuscript. Must be a duplicate.

Provide your synopsis and a cover letter containing your full contact information.

Thanks for considering LDP and Ca$h Presents.

Table of Content

MRBEATITUPRIGHT.com
By Eddie "Wolf" Lee

Romero

I'ma keep it three-hunnid wit'chu! Wit' the exception of homos, dope-fiends and crackheads, all niggas, regardless of race, age or religion, are addicted to three things: Money, power and pussy. And the only reason niggas be throwin' rocks at the penitentiary and takin' dirt naps at early ages for chasin' that paper and hood fame is to get as much pussy as possible.

So, in reality, the only thing ma'fuckas really are addicted to is *pussy!* Real shit! And yeah, for much of my life, I was one of those stupid niggas trappin' day and night and robbin' niggas for that sack just to floss in designer clothes and push foreign whips but most importantly, to get what's in between a bitch's thighs.

That twat, that monkey, that wet-wet, juice box, honey pot, sugar bowl, coochie, kitty kat, snatch, va jay-jay. But a nigga like me gon' keep it simple and call it what it is: pussy.

For as far back as I can remember, I had a thing for women. Black, White, Latina, Asian, thick, slim, curvy, fat. Wholesome, tomboy, gold digga. tall, short, amazon, midget, blind, cripple, ranging from ages eighteen to eighty. A nigga like me don't discriminate because I've always managed to find something sexy, alluring, captivating or intriguing about every bitch that crossed paths wit' me.

For example, her face might be jacked up but her ass is fat. Yeah, she's overweight, but she has a cute face and a heart of gold. Her ass flat as a board but her feet sexy as fuck. The bitch talk way too much but she can dress her ass off and her walk is mean. Or one of my pet peeves: The bitch is as dumb as a box of rocks but she's a go-getta and got a bangin' ass body from head-to-toe.

Bottom line, every bitch got something that's attractive about her. Sometimes you gotta pause and closely examine her exterior to find something physically attractive about her.

Other times you gotta completely disregard the physical, delve into her interior and find those mental attributes that are attractive. Trust me, no matter how fucked up a bitch's mug is, the minute you connect wit' her on a mental level, she'll start lookin' betta to you physically, too.

And don't get it twisted! Just 'cause I occasionally refer to women as bitches, don't mean I view *all* females as bitches, literally.

I was raised on the streets of Chi-raq, where the words *bitch* and *nigga* are commonly used as terms of endearment.

Anyway, where the fuck are my manners? I know my nigga, Wolf, wrote my name at the beginning of the story, but for y'all who don't know me personally, it's only right that I properly introduce myself. My name is Romero Woodley, but y'all can call me Ro-Ro. I'm a thirty-one-year-old, two-time felon and Black Disciple gang member, but my bangin' days are long behind me. I'm six-foot-three inches tall, two-hunnid twenty pounds of chiseled dark chocolate with a skilled tongue and a thick, ten-inch slightly curved dick that never fails to deliver toe-curlin', tear jerkin', painfully, yet pleasurable mind-blowin' orgasm after orgasm.

Bitches say I favor the singin', movie star nigga, Tyreese, and over the years a few niggas tried to test my get down because of the uncanny resemblance only to their detriment. But that's another story for a different book.

For the past three years, the only bangin' I've been doin' is between the sheets and the only thang I'm slangin' is dick. And the dick don't come cheap, either.

Shiid, looks ain't the only thing me and Baby Boy have in common. My clothes, jewelry, crib and fleet of cars are just as official as his, too. Real spit!

I got off that dumb shit and switched up my hustle while servin' time for armed robbery at

Stateville Correctional Center, a maximum-security joint in Joliet, Illinois.

I can vividly remember that shit like it was yesterday.

Clink! Clink! Clink!

The young Opie-lookin' correctional officer banged on my cell bars, wakin' me outta my sleep. "Woodley, get up and get dressed," he said, further pissin' me off.

"In the middle of the night!" I snapped

"For what? What time is it?" I demanded, irritated.

A nigga was locked down in segregation for twenty-three hours a day under investigation for stabbin' another inmate. Prison policy didn't allow inmates in seg to possess electronic devices, so I didn't know exactly what time it was.

"It's 2:30 and you got a mandatory healthcare call-pass to do some lab work. I'll be back to get you in ten minutes."

I started to say, "fuck you" and take my ass back to sleep, but I got up, took a piss, brushed my teeth and ran a hot rag over my face. Then I threw on my beige IDOC state-issued seg jumpsuit and slipped on my orange-colored rubber shower shoes.

Minutes later, the C/O returned. He cuffed my wrist, put leg irons around my ankles and fastened a steel chain around my waist. The chain was looped around the center of the handcuffs and leg irons and had a box and padlock attached to it for extra security measures.

After checkin' to make sure I was properly shackled, he slid open the cell bars and escorted me to the healthcare unit.

Once inside the healthcare building, I was taken to a secluded area that had a sign above the door that read: No Inmates Allowed Beyond This Point!

My antennas immediately went up.

"Real shit!" I barked wit' a scowl on my face, starin' dead into C/O's blue eyes. "I done already told you ma'fuckas I ain't did shit and I don't know shit. So, if this ain't 'bout no lab work, I suggest you take me back to my cell 'fore they be investigatin' what happened to yo' ass!" I threatened.

Shiiid, that ma'fucka didn't want no smoke. The entire prison staff knew my work. This was the third stabbin' I'd been investigated for.

The first two came from up under, and one of those was on a sergeant at another joint.

"Ay, man, I'm just following orders." Opie calmly replied as he opened the door. "The nurse is in this room, waiting to see you," he added, with a shit-eatin' smirk plastered across his face.

"Test me if you wanna," I said, then I stepped inside. Sittin' behind a desk was Lt. Diggins. The bitch was head of Internal Affairs. "Fuck naw!" I bellowed and turned to leave, but punk ass Opie quickly slammed the door shut.

Lt. Diggins stood up and smiled at a nigga. "Please have a seat," she said, sweetly.

Even though the bitch was I.A., every nigga on the yard thought she was feelin' them 'cause she was super-friendly to the point of being borderline flirty. A nigga like me was facing an attempt murder charge, so I wasn't stupid enough to think she was checkin' for me; however, I can't front, the broad was bad!

She favored Rihanna in the face, but had a body like Kim Kardashian. She didn't look a day over thirty, but judgin' by the five stars stitched on her officer's uniform, she had to be in her forties, each star represented five years on the job.

She kept smilin' at a nigga. "Please, have a seat," she

repeated, just as sweet.

Fuck it! I ain't have shit else to do, so I decided to humor myself.

"My story ain't changin' I already told you I don't know shit, but I'd rather sit in here wit' yo' fine ass than be locked in a cage any day." Unblushingly, I undressed her wit' my eyes before taking a seat.

"Wise decision." She shot me a sly grin as she sashayed over to the door, locked it, nodded at Opie and then pulled the shade down over the door's window.

"You sure it's safe for you to be locked in here alone wit'me?"

She turned, batted her lashes and seductively licked her lips. "I ain't scared of you." She strutted over to me. She then bent down and whispered in my ear, "If anything, you should be afraid of me."

My dick instantly rocked-up! "I 'on't know what type of games you playin', but if you as bad as you claim to be, take these shackles off me and we gon' see who should be scared of who."

I purposely leaned back so she could get an eyeful of this thick anaconda beggin' to be freed.

She looked at the pulsating imprint of my dick, bit down on her bottom lip and nodded approvingly.

"Be careful what you ask for 'cause you just might get it. But first things first." She picked up a folder off of the desk and waved it in my face. "I have three signed statements from inmates, including the victim, who all claim they witnessed you do the stabbing. Because you're a two-time felon, if convicted of attempted murder, you'd be hit with an enhancement and receive no less than thirty years in prison."

Listenin' to this bitch, not only did my dick go limp, I could barely stand the sight of her ass, but I wasn't 'bout to let her see me sweat. I kept a poker-face and continued listenin' to what she had to say.

"Now, luckily for you, two things I hate are snitches and sexy black men rotting away in a prison cell. You have two years left before you are released and if you agree to work for me when you get out and stay out of trouble the rest of your stay here, I promise you won't get charged for the attempted murder."

She really had my attention now. "Work for you? Doin' what?" I tried not to sound overly anxious.

She put the folder down and got directly in my face. "Do you like pussy?" She asked so close that our lips were practically touchin'. "And money?"

"Damn right! What nigga don't?"

"Are you secure wit' your sexuality and can you consistently please any woman, regardless of her physical attractiveness?"

"Take these shackles off and I'll show you betta than I can tell you!"

"Your wish is my command," she said, but before I could reply, her full, soft, gloss-covered lips were pressed up against mines. She stuck her mint-flavored tongue in my mouth and passionately kissed me before she got down on her

knees, unshackled me and stripped me butt-ass naked.

"Ain't no way I'm letting a body and cock like this go to waste," she purred, strokin' her small hand up and down the length of my thickness. She pulled out a Magnum, ripped it open wit' her teeth, placed the condom on her tongue, then inserted the head of my dick in her mouth.

Gazin' into my eyes, the freak bitch firmly gripped both my ass cheeks, and inch-by-inch pulled me into her mouth until the Magnum completely covered my shit.

"Yeah, that's right. Swallow this dick!" I encouraged her.

Due to my girth, most broads weren't able to effectively suck a nigga dick, but not this bitch. She was slurpin', moanin', deep throatin', sqeezin' my ass cheeks and starin' me in the face wit' them sexy ass hazel eyes the whole time she was doin' the damn thang.

"Oooooh! Shit! Yeah, like that!" I moaned, palmin' the back of her head. It had been six long years since I had a bitch's lips wrapped around my pole and I planned on enjoyin' the moment. "Ohhhhh! Ahhhh! Ohhhhhh! Shit! Yeah, that's right. Just like that!" I coaxed, feelin' my nut building.

Her slurpin' became sloppier. Her moans louder. She let go of my ass cheeks and grabbed my dick wit' one hand. Wit' the other one, she unfastened her pants and slid it down into her panties. She didn't miss a beat as she frantically worked her fingers in and out of her pussy while bobbin' her head back and forth on my dick.

This bitch was a beast! I closed my eyes 'cause the fuck-faces she was makin' was drivin' me crazy.

"Ooooh shit! Oh Shiiiit!" My dick began pulsatin'. My groin began tinglin'. A nut was bubblin' in my balls, ready to erupt. "Sssssss!" I hissed, but just as I was about to bust, she quickly pulled my dick out of her mouth and tightly squeezed both her hands around the shaft, just below the head, stoppin' a nigga from nuttin'.

"Not yet," she cooed.

"Oh, that's how you playin' it?" I smiled down at her 'cause I was gon' get my nut regardless, even if I had to beat my shit. "Don't tell me you a tease."

"Never that, Daddy." She kissed the tip of my chocolate stick. "I need you to fuck me! Can you do that?" she asked, all sexily and shit. "Can you make my pussy cum?"

The bitch had my joint throbbin'. "Damn right I can!"

She kissed my inner thigh, sending shock waves through my body. "My pussy dripping wet and I need to feel this long," she ran her tongue along the underside of my pole,"fat dick deep inside of me."

This bitch had a nigga fiendin' to bust her shit wide open. Due to our situation, her being a C/O and me an inmate, I allowed her to take control.

Nah, fuck that shit! I'm finna show this bitch. Matter fact, I'm finna dick this ho down for every nigga on the compound.

I snatched her ass up from off of the floor, pulled her pants and panties completely off, turned her around and bent her thick ass over the desk.

Her hips, perfectly round, caramel-colored ass and glistenin' pussy looked so good to a nigga that I had to taste it.

I squatted down, spread her voluptuous ass cheeks apart and licked from her clit, down her slit, all the way up the crack of her ass. I circled my tongue around the rim of her asshole, darted it in and out a few times and continued trailin' my tongue up her spine until I reached the nape of her neck.

Just like I figured, the bitch tasted delicious. "Hmmmmm!" I moaned in her ear, then I slipped my tongue in her mouth. She greedily accepted it, savorin' the fragrance and taste of her ass and pussy.

"You want me to fuck the shit outta you?" I whispered in her ear, rubbin' the tip of my dick up and down her slit.

"Yes! Yeeeeesss!" she squealed. "Put it in! Put it in!" she begged, reaching back for the dick. I swatted her hand away, prompting her to peer over her shoulder at a nigga. "Please. Beat this pussy up. Beat it up right!" she panted, lustfully. Without further delay, I pierced her opening. "Shit!" she cursed. "Take it slow, Daddy."

I barely had the head in and she was tryna climb to the other side of the desk.

"Naw, don't run!" I grabbed her tiny waist and held that ass in place. "You gettin' all this dick!" I declared and then I proceeded to methodically inch my way inside of her, until I was balls-deep.

Hands down, this bitch had the tightest, juiciest pussy my dick had ever been in. I started out wit' slow, shallow strokes, allowing her to adjust to a nigga size. She bit down on her bottom lip and took the dick like a champion.

"Oooh! Aahhh," she exhaled. Her pretty face was showin' a mixture of pain and pleasure. "Ohhh yes! Baby, yeess!" she moaned. "This pussy yours, Daddy. This pussy is all yours," she proclaimed, backin' that ass up. "That's right, Daddy, beat this pussy up!"

The smell of her sex. The sloshin' sounds of her pussy. Her moans of pleasure. The dirty-talkin' and sexy fuck-faces she made had a nigga on one-thousand tryna murder that pussy.

"Give me all this pussy." I grunted.

"Yes! Yes! Right there, Daddy. Right there. That's my spot! That's my spot!" she moaned, breathlessly, as I dicked her down. "Oooh shit! You 'bout to make me cum! I'm finna cum. I'm finna cum. Cum wit' me. Cum wit' meeeee!"

This bitch was drivin' me wild. I picked up my pace and lengthened my strokes. The super-wet pussy got wetter. Her inner thighs, pussy lips, the crack of her ass, my dick, balls and pelvis were covered wit' her nectar. I felt her sugar walls contractin' around my dick and a euphoric feelin' of ecstasy took hold of me.

Her body was shakin' and tremblin' in the throes of orgasmic bliss. I kept poundin' away like a man possessed.

"Oh shit! I cummin'. I'm cummin'. I'm cummmmminnnn!" she shrieked, as she orgasmed back-to-back.

The sight and sensation was too much for me to hold back. "Fuuuuck! Fuuuck! Arrrrrrgh!" I roared at the top of my lungs, releasing a long, thick hot stream of nut deep inside of her guts.

Exhausted and weak, I collapsed onto her back.

Whew! Gimme a minute. Thinkin' 'bout that pussy got my joint hard as steel.

Okay, after I blew Lt. Diggin's back out, she put on her clothes, then congratulated me, all bizness-like, on a job well done. I played along wit' the goofy shit and shook her hand.

C/O Opie, who stood outside of the door on look-out the entire time, put the shackles back on a nigga and took me back to seg.

A week later, I beat the Disciplinary Report and was back in general population.

I can't even front, though, a nigga was expectin' to hit that pussy again, but the shit never happened. Lt. Diggins was a real boss bitch!

For two straight years, I'd see her around the compound and she treated me the same way she did every other nigga in the joint, and so did Opie. But unlike most gossipin' ass niggas, I didn't go around braggin' and frontin'. I kept my mouth closed and a low profile the rest of my bid.

On my release date, when I got up to the front gate, a nigga was shocked to learn I had a ride waitin' on me in the parking lot and whoever it was sent an outfit inside for me to dress out in: A pair of Buscemi sneakers, True Religion jeans, Ferragamo belt, and a silk Polo V-neck t-shirt.

A nigga walked out of the joint fitted like a muthafucka! Then a platinum-colored G-wagon rolled up and stopped directly in front of me.

"Ro-Ro." A bad, young, high-yellow bitch wit' long hair rockin' a pair of Dolce & Gabbana shades called me by my nickname. “Get in.” She waved me around to the passenger side.

I jumped in and closed the door. “What’s good, Ma?” I asked, lickin’ my lips.

“Look, I know you just did eight and you thirsty as hell, but this ain’t that type of party!” The bitch immediately shut me down. But I ain’t give two fucks! Shiid, a nigga was happy to be out. Fuck that bitch!

On the ride back to the city, she told me Lt. Diggins had sent her to make sure I got home safely and that she had also brought the clothes I was wearing. Other than that, the stuck-up bitch didn’t say much else until she pulled up to the front of my building. She directed my attention to a Louis Vuitton duffel bag in the backseat.

“When you get out, take that wit’chu,” she said. “It’s six different pairs of designer pants and shirts, a pair of Mangiela and Balenciaga sneakers, and some Issy Miyake and Givenchy cologne inside it.” Then she reached into her purse and gave me $3,000, an iPhone and a piece of paper wit’ the phone’s number and passcode scribbled on it. “Do I need to explain where this shit came from?”

“Naw,” I said, unlocking the passenger door. “I ‘preciate the shit you bought me. Now, give me a kiss.” I leaned over but the boujetto bitch pulled back.

"I see you got jokes!" she capped. "But before you get out, lemme show you sumpin'. Pass me the cellphone."

She turned on the phone and held it in a position so that we could both see the screen. Next, she clicked on the Google App, typed in www.MRBEATITUP.com, and a website appeared wit' pictures of the singin' ass nigga, Tyreese, posin' in different clothes, positions, wit' his shirt off as well as stills of him from various movies he acted in.

"This is your personal website. Tomorrow a photographer gon' call you and set up a photo shoot. Lt. Diggins had the web designer put pictures of Tyreese on here so that you and the photographer can have a vision of the type of pictures and poses she wants. Soon as that's done, Tyreese pictures gon' be replaced wit' yours," she said.

"A'ight, cool," I replied, noddin' my head, but I ain't gon' lie, a nigga felt some type of way 'bout this shit. However, I kept it playa.

Next, she closed the website, logged into the phone's iCloud, and showed me my email address. All this shit was foreign to a nigga so I paid close attention.

"This email account is strictly fo' bizness. When a client requests your services, she'll email you personally and tell you exactly what she wants, how she wants it and when and where she wants you to meet her. And, just so you know, Lt. Diggins pre-screens every client before they contact you."

Shiid, I hear the bitch talkin', but she ain't said a word about that paper. "How much these bitches payin' and how I'm supposed to get the money?" I asked, 'cause I ain't 'bout to let no bitch, regardless if she can send me back to prison for thirty years, pimp me.

"Dang, calm down. I was finna get to that next," the bitch said, rollin' her eyes. Like I gave a fuck! Then she showed me how to access a Paypal account. "Now, by the time the client emails you, she done already agreed to a certain price negotiated by Lt. Diggins. Once you send the client the confirmation email, your cut, which will be 60% of the negotiated fee, will be deposited into this Paypal account."

"Sixty-percent," I repeated, sourly.

"Yeah, nigga," she said in true ghetto fashion. "The mini-mum fee is $3,000. That's just fo' a date and/or regular sex. If she got fantasies and other freaky shit she wanna do, that fee can go through the roof!"

"Okay, we'll see," I said as I hopped out the SUV. I opened up the rear door, got the duffel bag out and dipped my head back in. "How I'm 'pose to get up wit' Ms. Diggins?" A nigga wasn't in the joint no more. That lieutenant shit was dead wit' me.

"Oh yeah, thanks fo' remindin' me." The bitch looked at me and smiled for the first time. "Under no circumstances are you to ever try to contact Lt. Diggins. If you do, it'll be hell to pay. She has all your info, so if she needs to holla, she'll contact you."

Long story short, I shut her door and I ain't seen or heard from that bitch or Ms. Diggins since, and that was three years ago. But the hustle is real! I don't know where Ms. Diggins findin' these overpaid/undersexed professional bitches at, but I been takin' down three to four of 'em a week, makin' no less than $5,400, and that ain't including gifts, trips and tips.

Hold up. A nigga just got an email alert.

From: awhitelesbiancravingblackdick

Hello, Mr. Beatitupright, my name is Amy Lynn. I'm a 5'2", 112 pound, true blonde (picture attached) that's been faithfully married to my beautiful wife for 5 years. However, the dildo hasn't been enough for me lately. For the past few months, I've been masturbating to pictures of you on your website and pretending my wife was you when she fucks me with the strap-on. I have a fantasy that you (and only you) can make me cum true, but the window of opportunity is slim because my wife is always around. However, she'll be out of the house for the next six hours. So, I need you to get here A.S.A.P! My fantasy is for you to come into my bedroom wearing a ski-mask and black gloves and flat-out rape me. I want you to fuck me in the ass and force me to suck your big black cock afterward. My address is 555. N... The front door will be unlocked and a pair of gloves and a ski-mask will be on the floor outside my bedroom door. I'll be asleep waiting.

Lemme see what she looks like, not that it matters.

Damn! This sexy ma'fucka look like the Jennifer Aniston back in her Friends days. Yeah, I'm finna slay this freak-nasty bitch.

I'm off to handle mines. Too bad y'all horny ma'fuckas gonna hafta wait to read about how I'ma beat that ass up right.

The End

You, Me and She
By Juicy

"Hello," Cherelle answered seductively when she seen Drew's number display across the screen.

"Yes, I'm returning the message you left for Drew. Can I help you with something?" the female questioned.

Cherelle was surprised to hear a woman's voice instead of Drew's but she remained unfazed and cool as a cucumber just the same, "Sure, you can tell Drew that I called."

"I can do that, but can you tell me what this about first?" she spoke impatiently.

"I could but he already knows so just have him return my call. Thank you."

No sooner than Cherelle ended the call, her phone rang again from Drew's number but yet a different voice spoke. This voice was more emotional than the last.

"Hi Cherelle, my name is Keturah, that was my cousin Eboni who just called you and Drew is my fiancé," she outwardly stated. "I'm sorry I didn't just come direct but I figured I could get more information the other way."

"Well you can see that initial stunt didn't work. Listen, I can respect your honesty now but before you go off into details and begin asking twenty one questions, refer them to him. He's your man." Cherelle said bluntly.

"I know this isn't your problem but he won't tell me the truth," she admitted.

"And you don't know me, so what makes you feel I would?" Cherelle remarked.

"I don't know but I was hoping that woman to woman you would understand," she reasoned. "We have a baby together and we have been in a relationship for three years. You're not the fist girl that I've found out about but he would lie about their dealings and if I was able to talk to them they sided with his story. I'm just asking you to be different." Keturah pleaded.

Her words weren't that compelling but something inside Cherelle felt sympathy, sisterly compassion even. She knew Drew long enough to make him a regular but because he thought so little of her to be forthcoming about his engagement she opted to be real with her. Cherelle was straight to the point. She explained how they met and the nature of their sexship. Keturah sat quietly on the other end of the line and listened closely. Once Cherelle finished Keturah let out a heavy sigh, then she followed up with a light whimper.

"So did Drew make plans to see you anytime soon?"

"It doesn't work like that, we're not dating. If I am in the mood for company or vice versa, we'll holla."

"I see," Keturah hesitated for a while, "do you think you can make plans to see him?"

"And what good would that do for you?" Cherelle asked.

"It would provide me with proof."

"Proof?" Cherelle uglied her face, "How much more proof do you need? I just told you the truth."

"Would you believe what another woman was telling you about your man? I just need to know for myself now, know what I mean?"

"Then why ask me to begin with if you were gonna doubt me in the end? And how 'bout I flip the script. Who's to say that you're his woman? You could be an admirer trying to get where you fit," Cherelle turned the tables.

"I'll call you from my phone when he comes home. Please answer."

"Whatever," Cherelle surmised before terminating the conversation.

A few hours passed and an unknown number was calling Cherelle's cell. She assumed correctly when she figured it was Keturah. She sure nuff heard her having a conversation with Drew but she still wasn't convinced that they were an item until she brought up their wedding plans and he chimed in, throwing his thoughts on the guest list and sorts. Cherelle wasn't the least upset about them being together, because they weren't an item. All that connected them was the bump n grind. After hearing enough of the "baby I love yous" she disconnected the call and lied down.

Early the next morning her phone rung and it was yours truly.

"You're beginning to call me more than your man. What do you want now?" Cherelle snapped.

"I deserve that," Keturah mentioned before disregarding it. "I'm not trying to be a bother but I just want to know if you'll give me the evidence that I desire since you know that all is official between Drew and I?"

"I didn't owe you the thirty minute conversation yesterday and I don't owe you this. If you gotta go through all this searching and scheming, leave 'em. And if you love him too much to bounce, then stay with him. But don't involve me in your scam," Cherelle stated clearly.

"Have you ever been in love? I mean seriously?" Keturah asked. Cherelle said nothing. "Well love will make you do some crazy things and this is one of mine. I feel empty when he's away and whole when he's near me. As much as my head says to believe you, my heart tells me that I need more then that before I can walk away. I won't have peace knowing that Drew could possibly be with you if what you say is true unless you can give me the confirmation I need to set myself free."

"And all you want is to hear him with me so you'll know for certain that he's fooling around?" Cherelle questioned.

"In a nutshell, yes."

"Okay, I'll give you that. The next time I see him, I will call you and hopefully you'll spread your wings and fly because you can't make a rolling stone stand still."

"Thanks Cherelle."

"Bye Keturah."

Later in the week Drew called Cherelle to make plans to see her for the weekend. She obliged as always and like clockwork he was at her door. Cherelle debated on whether she should really betray him by liberating her but what the hell Drew was replaceable, especially since she learned he wasn't as up front about things as she thought. She never gelled well with liars anyhow. Cherelle called her. Keturah sat silently on the phone listening carefully to her soon-to-be tell another woman how much he missed spending time with her, how special she was to him but more shocking, how he was falling for her. Keturah's breath became short as she gasped to replace the air that quickly deflated her lungs. She sat like a zombie in limbo. She wanted to shatter her phone to pieces but couldn't free the grip that kept her linked to her gut wrenching pain.

Beep…

"No—No—No," Keturah whispered into the receiver. "I need to know—," Beep… "more," she said defeated right as Cherelle's cell phone died.

Keturah loved Drew more than keeping her sanity and as much as she felt that verbal confirmation could convince her to step, she couldn't pick up her feet to walk in the front door's direction. She rocked back and forth on the sofa trying to make sense of why her man was with another woman when he should have been there with her. Keturah had to see Cherelle, she had to know what she had on her, and she had to win back what was supposed to be hers already.

The next day, Keturah called Cherelle and at this point Cherelle kind of expected it.

"Yeah," Cherelle answered.

"I just called to say that I heard Drew."

"Good for you," Cherelle said.

"But," she paused, "I thought that hearing him there with you would be enough ammo for me to fiyah his ass but after hearing him tell you all those profound things only made me wonder. What else is he willing to do to me behind my back?"

"Everything!"

"Okay but part of me still feels that he's just being a man talking to you for whatever reason and that he truly loves me," she stressed.

"But we do more than talk and I told you that in our first…," Cherelle threw her hand in the air, "let me guess you're not certain if I'm telling the truth so you have to know that too for yourself, right?"

"As bogus as it sounds I do need to know," Keturah's voice dropped.

"This is wild on so many levels but I guess you want to be on the phone for that as well?"

"No, this I need to see in person with my own eyes."

Cherelle's mouth dropped. She heard of some crazy in love women doing some off the wall things but never to this degree. Never in her illest dream would she have imagined a woman purposely serving her man up on a sexual platter.

"So you want me to invite you over to my place before Drew arrives as you watch your worst fears materialize in the worst way? Take my word. He's a cheater, "Cherelle offered.

"That's the problem, I can't," Keturah contended, "last night hurt but my heart can mend from that. Confirmation of that magnitude forces me to see him for who he is."

Cherelle saw that befriending Drew meant dating his fiancé and that was one threesome that she wanted no parts of, so to rid them both she decided to give Keturah exactly what she wanted. Although she grew accustomed to Drew's lovemaking, no man was worth the confusion. So they arranged a time in which Keturah would have the verification that she so frantically needed.

After several weeks of uncoordinated schedules and other mishaps they were able to agree on a time. Keturah made arrangements for their daughter to spend the weekend by her grandma's house and she told Drew that she would be out with the girls all night. He had no problem with that because he too made plans to be out all night and she knew why, because in essence they had the same agenda in mind which was to meet by Cherelle's. Cherelle instructed Keturah to make it for seven but in a rush to beat him out the door she left without her credit card and she didn't put enough gas in her car to make it out to New Orleans' East. So midway there upon her discovery she had to double back to get her wallet and fuel unless she intended on staying longer than expected. She arrived at Cherelle's apartment behind schedule but she noticed that Drew hadn't, he was already there.

"Damn-it!" Keturah shouted in her vehicle. She dialed Cherelle's number.

"Yep," Cherelle coolly answered.

"Sorry, had a delay. Is there any way you can sneak me in?" she whispered.

"Doubt it. You're too late. I already have company." Cherelle played it off.

"Bae, tell that nigga you 'bout to be real busy," Drew said out loud as he kicked off his shoes and stretched across her bed.

"Cherelle figure out a way, please." Keturah pouted.

"I can't," she said bluntly, turning away. "Maybe next time you'll come before he does." Cherelle then powered her phone off.

Keturah frowned and looked at the flashing "call ended" message before she redialed instantly but she only got her voicemail. She sat in her car from a distance still able to see the window of the room that she assumed belonged to her go out in less than five minutes. She was floored but even that indication wasn't enough for her to believe. What she did believe was that some things aren't what they seem. It didn't apply in this case but that is what got her through this episode. Drew came out close to one o'clock in the morning. He jetted down the stairs of her third story apartment and hopped in his truck. She thought to knock on her door, give Cherelle the once over, check for the scent of sex, but she choose to tail him instead just in case he had another run on his schedule. He actually went straight home and she parked a block away from her usual spot. She dialed Cherelle's number and this time her phone was on.

"Umm hmm," Cherelle unintentionally sounded seductive.

"You were cold as ice, not letting me in and turning off your phone on me," Keturah said sharply.

Cherelle sat up in her bed, "What did you expect me to do? You're taking this 'sisters gotta stick together' crap to a whole 'notha level. I'm not responsible for helping chics bring their stray men home. I'm a single mama trying to get me. So with that in mind anything past me telling," she stressed, "the truth which I didn't have to do, is way more than I should have done. You got me breakin' all kinds of G codes with your obsessive need to confirm what you already know to be a fact."

Keturah sat back in her seat and listened to another woman put her in her place. Cherelle was right, she's the other woman and she didn't owe her a damn thing. If she would have picked a better man maybe she wouldn't be playing detective but instead be at home with her man playing doctor.

"My bad. I'm vexed and I'm just hurt, I need to get this over with. My imagination is getting the best of me."

"What's there to imagine. He just spent close to six hours with me. Do you honestly believe we were asleep? Honey he has his own bed for that. The nigga broke me off but you're so hell bent on seeing for yourself that tonight means nothing to you."

"It's not that, if I confront him now, he'll lie his way out and then he'll be more cautious with you. I want to catch him in the act with his pants down." Keturah rationalized.

"Well you get here early enough next time and that's exactly how you'll see him. Good night Keturah," Cherelle hung up her phone but then decided to cut it off again just in case she called in the morning.

Unbelievably it had been a few days since Cherelle talked to Keturah. But she knew as long as she fixated on Drew's whereabouts she would be popping up soon. "Bug a Boo" started chiming from her cell and she laughed because that was the ring tone that she assigned to her.

"Ha ha ha, what is it?" Cherelle answered.

Keturah wanted to ask her what was funny but didn't see the point. "Drew just called me at work and said that he'll be working overtime. I doubt that seriously because they recently had cut backs. Was he feeding me an alibi because he's really coming to see you?"

"Actually he is."

"What time?" Keturah asked.

"Within the hour."

"Damn it! I'll still be at work."

"My man being at another chic's house would be my red flag," Cherelle scoffed.

"I know I look like a fool to you. I feel like one but at least I'm being true to myself. I know he comes by and spends lots of time with you but like I said I still need to know beyond a shadow of a doubt that he's stepping out."

"Have it your way, I'll call you this time and maybe after hearing some porn radio, you'll be satisfied," Cherelle volunteered.

"Cherelle, it's not that I get a thrill out of this. It tears me apart each time that I feel as if I am spoon feeding him to you. I can't stop him but at least I can put to rest the idea of him and I being Mr. and Mrs. Richard once I bust him in action."

"Oh I believe that it's torture, I just don't understand how you can endure so much of it but you'll get what you ask for," Cherelle stated.

"Cherelle, I almost forgot. Please make sure your phone is charged. It died the last time."

"Whatever," Cherelle hung up.

Cherelle soaked in her tub of bubbles. She shaved her velvety smooth skin and hairs off of Ms. Snapper. She moisturized her entire body before applying Drew's favorite perfume. She went back in forth with what to wear. Something barely there or nothing at all, she opted to go with that sexy number he picked up for her as a birthday gift to himself early that year. Cherelle looked good enough to eat and that's exactly what Drew was gonna conclude when he saw her as well. She was all set to give Keturah an ear's full. Less than an hour passed and Drew knocked. She called Keturah and she placed her phone on mute as Cherelle set her on speaker phone, placing her cell on the nightstand. Drew walked in her bedroom.

"Damn, you smell editable," he noted as he sat down.

She propped her foot onto her bed revealing the crotch less panties she was wearing, "I taste even better."

He slid one finger. Two fingers inside of her fiyahlicious treat. He ran his fingers across his nose and inhaled deeply before he sucked them bone dry. He slapped her fat posterior and kissed her pearl before he got on his knees and ate her voraciously as she stood.

"Oh Drew, I'm gonna come in your mouth," she mentioned as she slowly grinded her come back.

Without detaching his lips from hers, he quickly removed his pants and started beating his meat to discharge his premies. He felt the sprays of her waterfall drench his face as he oozed his own cascade.

She crawled in bed like a sex kitten. She told him that she wanted him to describe the feel and what he's doing as he was doing it. Grabbing at Lil Big Drew he agreed.

"First prediction of the night, I'ma give you multis," he boasted.

"Multiple orgasms huh? Show and tell."

He rolled on a raincoat, "Stand to your feet, spread 'em and touch the floor."

She bent over, "What's next?" she asked as she felt him glide his fingers over her juices spreading it over her exit only.

He tapped her rear-end with his joy stick a few times, "I'm 'bout to blow your back out!" He peeked the tip inside as if to test the temperature of her waters before he dived in. He pulled out, "Now you see it," he shoved it in, "now you don't." Drewdini worked her over with his dick disappearing act. He moistened his finger and as he slid himself back into her, he placed his lubricated digit into her asshole. She moaned out in exxstasy.

"Dis my pussy and my ass," he declared.

"Fuck me, Drew! Fuck me harder," she bucked on his stallion.

He smacked her ass again. "Walk to the couch and lean over the armrest," he commanded.

She stood upright and walked slowly, careful not to free her captive. She did as she was told; forgetting about Keturah's need to listen as she was then concerned about her own. She draped the arm of the sofa as he commanded. He loved watching her perfectly shaped dunk jump from behind with each thrust of "The Punisher." The way she took all of him not backing him away like Keturah drove him insane. He divided her cheeks exposing her hypnotic device before he lost himself inside her again. This time he pounded so hard that her sofa began moving from its original place. He pulled her hair, forcing her head to go backwards as he pressed deeper in. He smacked her with his free hand watching it shake like jello. He placed his foot on her cushion to give him a different angle in her ill na na.

"That's all you got?" she taunted, knowing this brought out the beast in him.

"Fuck no!" he breathed heavily as he pulled himself out and rubbed her wetness along the trail of her anus. He dipped his thickly shaped penis into Ms. Snapper before easing his Oscar Meyer sausage in between her bumper. She cried out from the initial pain as he continued his stretch.

"Talk some more shit," he enticed.

She couldn't, she was turned on to the max and unable to do anything but moan. He hammered in her with a vengeance as he toyed with her twat with three exploring fingers. So turned on by his bad girl he shot off instantly. Contracting her muscles around his fingers she creamed as well. He removed himself from her back-door and kissed her sweet bottom. He slipped into her bathroom to run a hot shower for them as she went back to her room. She picked up her phone and seen that Keturah wasn't there.

Cherelle text her, "Did you hear it?"

Moments later Cherelle got a response, "Hell no! My manager caught me off of break. Another time."

Fine with her, she thought. In the meantime, she decided to give Drew more of her unforgettable.

Keturah couldn't clock out fast enough before she dialed Cherelle. Cherelle picked up, "How much did you hear?"

"Nothing really, all I heard was you moanin' for a few seconds."

Cherelle was in shock at how that wasn't enough. "Okay, I am dying to hear you reason this one out. Let me hear it," she berated.

"For all I know you could have had a good massage, that's what it sounds more like, to be truthful."

"So in other words what you're saying is that I don't have anything better to do with my time, than to perform for you," Cherelle sucked in her teeth. "At first I felt a little sorry for you but now this is straight comic view to me because everything that comes out your mouth is laughable. Admit that you're either a glutton for pain or the synapses in your brain aren't working properly."

"It ain't any of that," Keturah said offended. "You don't have the right to judge me!"

"I'm not judging. I'm just telling it like it is. Drew knows that if you find a sucka, you lick it. And that's all he's doing. So if you want to put an end to this, do your math. Drew plus me equals cheating on you. Add it up; it's all there for you. Now subtract yourself and you're minus the heartache that way when Drew divides his time with everybody else, 'cause he will, you won't feel like you're two times the loser."

"You feel like you got the upper hand or something because I keep coming to you like this? He may be with you on some level but he returns to me, the one he wants his future with."

"Then your future isn't that bright. I don't have ups on you. That isn't what this is about. I'm just asking you to deal with the real. If you want to know the facts then quit denying them. And calm your ass down too because the way it looks, the only one who's on your side isn't the one who should be. Understand that or do I need to spell it out for you?"

"Ever heard the saying, 'Keep your enemies close'? That's what you could be doing under the disguise that you're helping me out but really all you want is my man."

"You sound ridiculous. You're on the phone with me now because I have your man. A fraction, a piece, a smidgen, doesn't matter how much, but I do. And let me set the record straight, I'm not the enemy because you're already sleeping with him. I didn't know you existed and if memory serves me right, I was willing to step away but you wanted all this. You needed proof!"

Keturah said nothing as she fought back the urge to go off but if she did that then she would for real be the next contestant on the Guessing Game.

"Look Cherelle, my beef isn't with you. If you can make sure that he's at your place, I will be there too. And we can be out of each other's hairs."

"Whatever." Cherelle retorted before pressing the end button.

Two more weeks passed and D-day arrived. Keturah finally met the woman that was the cause of her many sleepless nights. Cherelle welcomed her in her home moments before Drew was to show up. Keturah eyed Cherelle and her insecurities heightened. Cherelle was beautiful and although Keturah was a slim bombshell something about Cherelle made her feel incomparable to her. Maybe because she had her man faithfully coming back to her punani and she couldn't get her man to simply be faithful. Or maybe because Cherelle was a full figured sistah with curves like a wavy road, her mahogany skin was flawless except for the small scar above her lip which oddly added to her natural stunning looks. Cherelle's eyes resembled Nefertiti and the more Keturah tried to find imperfections, she only discovered that she's was an exotic beauty who could rightfully attract any man including her own. Keturah sat opposite of the woman she hoped to make out a liar by the end of the evening but something in her soul told her that she wouldn't. The more they talked the more she began to realize that she didn't really want to know after all but before she could change her mind and live in the comfortable shadows of ignorance, Cherelle's doorbell rang.

"You're either brave or you're stupid but either way you're about to be put on some game. Do not come out of hiding under any circumstances. You are to watch only until I walk out."

Keturah shook her head with complete understanding that she was definitely the latter. Only a fool would do something like this but it was too late to renege now. She took her place in Cherelle's walk in closet as she held her breath anticipating what was to come.

Without any delay in getting the show on the road, Cherelle walked Drew in her room and began to undress herself. Drew followed suit and removed his clothing as well. Keturah couldn't believe that not only was he there but without words he instinctual followed her lead. There was no hesitation in his movement, he didn't ponder whether he should stop, and he conveniently forgot he was involved because he was gung ho. Cherelle laid on her bed and licked her two index fingers erotic like before she gently inserted them in her passion fruit. She maneuvered her free hand over her melons and gave Drew the *come to mama* look. She lustfully watched him stand at the foot of the bed with his penis jumping eagerly like a spring chicken. He positioned himself to partake of her yum and she spread eagle to give him full passage. He smoothed over her soft and voluptuous thighs placing her legs on his shoulders as his head disappeared between her goodies. Keturah gasped as she saw Drew hungrily eat her with the same mouth that kissed hers just that morning. Keturah slid down onto her hands and knees and covered her mouth to muffle her cry. She glanced out the crack in the door and gagged once she saw Cherelle faced down with her laffy taffy in the air and his tongue gliding between the split of her brown round. He moaned out as he dipped his candy licker back into her bowl of cherries. Cherelle clutched her pillow tightly as tiny bolts of electricity shot through her body. Her back curved as he circled around her joy hole. She turned over on his command and her eyes gravitated towards his golden rod then his bedroom eyes then onto Keturah's widened teary eye peeping from the closet. And though Cherelle knew Keturah had seen enough to conclude that he most definitely was a double dealer she decided that the show must go on.

Cherelle curved her pointing finger towards her face and like a puppy Drew obeyed and crawled on top of her. She breastfed him, he stroked his man, she threw her head back and he said, "I want you—now."

With no further ado, she tore open a condom and he placed it on his shaft. Positioning himself missionary style he lowered onto and inside her divine and upon entry he cried out in pleasure. Keturah started to tremble as she watched the makings of her world come crashing down in front of her. She wanted to barge out the door and put a stop to it all but she wasn't prepared to meet up with Cherelle's friend Nina whom rested on her nightstand. She had no other choice but to suffer through what seemed like the beginning of a long and torturous night.

He slipped in and out of her milky way, passionately holding her in his embrace. Cherelle almost felt like he knew it would be their last time the way he meticulously moved faster then slower, stroking deeper than he's ever gone while shoveling his strong hands underneath her ass to bring their two bodies closer than close. Suddenly Drew's arms stiffened and his back straightened like an arrow as he welcomed the unloading of his cannon with his last push inside Cherelle's slippery heaven. Rolling over onto his side, he smiled graciously at the hefty deposit that saturated his jimmy. Keturah was breathless but relieved that it was over and her moment of confrontation was vastly approaching, but Cherelle didn't give her the signal, she didn't move. Instead Drew opened Cherelle's goodie drawer and retrieved some items. He pulled out the soft cuffs, edible dusting powder and another condom. Keturah's eyes were burning from the tears she cried over the last hour and a half, her muscles were achy from being so tensed up and now her nose was dripping tiny beads of blood from the overwhelming levels of stress she was currently under. Her temperature was though the roof and she was feeling light headed from her elevated pressure and to add more insult she now was about to witness an encore.

Cherelle stretched his body across her bed placing his hands above his head connected to her bed rail. She also reached and grabbed her blind fold just to ensure that he didn't raise his head and notice that another set of eyes were watching. She covered her breast with the cotton candy flavored powder and then straddled his raging bull to begin part two of her taboo. Cherelle began to ride him slowly, contracting her muscles around his silky pole. His toes curled then unfolded with each drop of her bodacious booty greeting the base of his dick. She leaned forward and placed her perfectly perky titties in his salivating mouth. He began to lose control and begged Cherelle to untie him so that he can hold her but she refused. Unable to control his speech he screamed, "I love…,"

"Who nigga? Who the fuck do you love?" Keturah yelled, surprising Cherelle moments before she knocked her out cold with the butt of the same gun she threatened to use if she had gotten out of line. He heard the thud of his temptress body hit the floor.

"What the hell? Keturah!" Drew called out. Unable to see a thing or move his upper body, he froze with fear.

"I loved you while you loved this bitch. Now you can die with her."

Bang…Bang…Bang…

The sound of the headboard banging against the wall brought Keturah back from her crazed fantasy just in time to hear her man finish his sentence.

"…dis pussy. I love dis pussy."

Umm was all that escaped her lips. She positioned herself on her feet and popped on his dick like she was dancing to a Luke throwback. Each time Keturah saw his light caramel wand disappear then reappear from inside her magic place her heart skipped beats.

"Oh, baby ooh, I'm 'bout to explode," Drew announced.

"I'm about to come with you baby."

Suddenly she coated him with her aqua fina and he bust his gun at the same time. Their love making was so intense that from the look of things, they seemed to be more of a couple than cutty buddies. Soon Drew's breathing regulated and Cherelle freed his wrists. She French kissed him as if she didn't want to leave the moment, grabbed her silk robe that draped her bed post, her handgun and slipped out her room singing Rihanna's song, "But it's over now, go on and take a bow…"

"Bring me a warm and soapy towel baby," he ordered.

He lay in the bed with his eyes closed and his hands behind his head, while scissor kicking the sheets. Keturah slowly approached Drew. Her nerves had her shook. With no other plan or recourse, she stretched her hand as far back as she could and sent it crashing down on his cheek.

"Cher…" he yelped.

"No nigga, Keturah," she slapped him again, "your fucking fiancé." She attempted to strike him once more but he caught her hand. She tried with the other but he grabbed that one too.

"What tha? How tha hell?" Drew managed to ask as he restrained Keturah's wild movement.

"What the hell are you doing, fucking another woman, Drew?" she screamed at top of her lungs.

"I—I can explain baby," Drew let go of her as he stumbled over himself trying to step into his boxers. "This only happened because I was missing you!"

"Bullshit, nigga! You were getting your jollies off thinking I would never find out about it. I defended you against everyone's accusations, even my own but I see the truth now. I hate you and I want you gone tonight!"

"Wait a minute," Drew demanded, standing inches from Keturah who was crying profusely with sweat forming at her brow. "Every time I tried making love to my kitkat, you'd tell me you were too tired from work, the baby, whatever. I wasn't cheating to leave you. I did this so that I can get a release but still stay."

Keturah's words became shaky and unconvincing, "I'm done and we through."

Cherelle listened at the door and admired Keturah's strength. She honestly didn't think she had it in her to kick his lying ass to the curb.

"You don't mean that. You're upset baby."

"I'm beyond upset. I am pissed off! And you…"

Drew held her close and told her that he can only love one woman. How Cherelle was a mistake and that he needed a chance to make it right. The more she wrestled to get away from his hold, the firmer he held her, she was trapped. He kept whispering in her ear to not let his stupid man actions ruin all the good times.

"I'm sorry, angel," a tear dropped from his eye and rolled unto her cheek. "I understand that what I did was unforgivable but I am asking you to look within and remember that I'm still Drew, the man that would give you his last everything—including name."

Keturah's was confused. She was crossed between wanting to rip out his heart and wanting to kick herself in the behind for bringing this all on herself. But she said nothing as he continued.

"Let's go home—please." Drew genuinely begged. Separating himself from her he uttered, "Please."

A few moments later, Cherelle didn't hear anything so she pushed her door open slightly just to discover that the iron machine Keturah started off as turned into soft putty. Cherelle laughed a little before she opened her door completely.

"It's time that y'all two leave my house and never return," she waved her nine in the direction of the front door.

“I’ll make everything up to you, I promise. Just don’t leave me baby,” he whined, putting on his clothes not taking his eyes off of Keturah.

And just like that Keturah forgave him without saying a word. After the oohs and aahs, the used condoms, the whole damn shebang, she disregarded it because he said he loved her? But who did he just show her he loved? Himself.

Drew walked past Cherelle and shot a wicked smile as if to cockily say, “I can’t be stopped, this is Drew, baby,” with Keturah’s hand in his leading her through the house. Keturah hung her head in shame trailing behind him but Cherelle grabbed her free hand, jerking her body to face her.

“You went through all of this just to leave with him as if you didn’t see shit?” Cherelle scoffed in disbelief.

“Have you ever been in love?” Keturah whispered to her before Drew pulled her out the door.

Cherelle shook her head as she closed her door and thought, *If I would have known that in the end ole girl was gonna keep him anyway, I would have kept him too.*

Wet and Juicy
By Kameelah Parker

MONAE

As soon as I stepped out of the shower, I grabbed my towel off of the counter to dry off. I stood there in the mirror admiring my body, something I did often. However, this time it was much deeper, as if I had an out-of-body body experience.

It had been three months since Devin had left to go back to DC and I was feening for his dick. Devin had decided to take a teaching job in DC because they paid him more than they did here in North Carolina.

We agreed that once we found a tenant to rent out our home, I would move there with him; however, it had been a year and six months since he'd been away.

I wasn't happy about Devin taking the job offer and not having him home every night was frustrating, but I tried to be as supportive as possible and not show my unhappiness. I usually did well coping with the change, until those days came when I needed to feel him inside of me.

Damn, I miss my baby.

Every time I thought about how big, black, thick and juicy his dick was and how he always stroked me just right, my pussy would throb, which would happen whenever I was in great need of a quick fix.

I had gotten so familiar with the feeling of longing that I named it *the pussy heartbeat* and most of the time taking a cold shower would do the trick, calming me just long enough to get my need satisfied, but this night, in particular, I had taken two cold showers and it still would not stop beating.

I had promised myself I would not cheat on my husband again, but it seemed as though the longer he stayed away, the harder it became.

Man, fuck, I can't take this shit!

I stood there in the mirror, staring at the roundness of my nipples and how perky my titties were. I closed my eyes for a split second, while taking my right pointer finger into my mouth, inserting it in and out slowly. All the while using my left hand to caress my titties.

Slowly, I imagined me sucking Devin's dick.

"Uuuummmm," I moaned, leisurely pushing my finger in and out of my hot and salivating mouth.

I knew it was only a matter of minutes before my sweet wetness would come running down my legs like melted ice cream ran down the side of a cone. Nothing made me wetter than sucking dick. I craved it, I needed it, I loved that shit.

Walking into my bedroom, I laid back onto the bed, reached over and opened the drawer to my nightstand pulling out the biggest dick I owned. I then used the same finger that was inside of my mouth to massage my clit, stroking it in a circular motion.

Going ‘round and ‘round until I felt myself jerk, I spoke just above a whisper. “Shit!”

I quickly inserted the dildo into my wet puss, slowly grinding my hips up and down on it, making sure to fill my insides up completely.

Going as deep as I possibly could, I felt a warm sensation come rushing over me. “Ahhhhhhh! Dammmnnn!”

After cumming so quickly, I wanted to cum again.

I had bought so many sex toys to help me during my time of need when Devin was away, but I used them so often that they never measured up to the real thing. I got pleasure from sucking the dildo off, but it was something about how Devin’s brick hard dick would swell inside of my jaws while I was slowly using my mouth walls to suck his soul out of him. I was addicted to dick sucking, and I knew it.

Who the hell can I call? I thought as I laid there in the bed looking up at the ceiling.

I grabbed my phone off of my nightstand and scrolled through my contacts. I dialed my ex's number. Cameron and I had dated for a year until I found out he was having an affair with someone else. After the relationship was over, we still remained friends and had messed around from time to time. He didn't take the news too well when he found out I had started a serious relationship with Devin, but that was his problem.

I know this nigga gon' answer the phone," I told myself.

When the voicemail came on, I hung up and sent a message instead.

I know you probably still mad at me but I need to see you. I miss you.

I waited five minutes for him to respond, but just as I thought, no response.

"Well, fuck you, nigga!" I uttered, throwing my phone on the bed while getting up to go wash up a bit and throw on a pair of panties.

It was only 9 p.m. and I was no way near sleepy. My boredom turned into frustration, which led me to becoming mad at Devin all over again.

"Why would he really leave me here? This shit is getting depressing." I huffed and poured me three shots of Patron.

Standing in the middle of the kitchen, struggling to get both shots down, I noticed China Garden's menu posted on the side of the fridge.

"M*aybe I should just order me some wings and look at Netflix till I fall asleep.*"

As soon as I took one step toward the room, the doorbell rang, scaring the living shit out of me. "*Who the hell is this at the door?*"

I wasn't expecting anyone over and was totally blown to think who could possibly be at my house unannounced at this time of the night. I crept quietly toward the front door and grabbed the bat from inside of the coat closet, gripping the door knob with one hand, holding the bat in the other all the while holding my head down with my ear to the door.

"Who is it?" I yelled.

"It's Riq, Mo."

"Who?" I asked again, wanting to make sure I heard the name correctly.

"Riq!" he shouted firmly.

"O*h shit!*" I totally forgot that Tariq had called stating he would be coming by after work to pick up his clippers that he had let Devin use a couple of weeks ago. I quickly unlocked the door to find him standing outside of the screen door.

"Give me a minute. I'll go grab them." Unlocking the screen door, I ran to the back to grab my robe and the clippers. I heard the door shut as I rushed to put my robe on.

"So, you forgot or you just acting like you forgot?" Riq asked as soon as I came back into the living room.

Tariq was looking good, as usual, with his dark skin and sparkling white teeth. He always wore a fade, which accented his beard that connected to his goatee. He never left the house without his fitted hat that he wore over his sexy bedroom eyes.

"I really forgot, Riq." I handed him the clippers, looking down at the floor, grabbing the side of my neck and trying not to make eye contact.

"Yea, I hear you," he spat back, and then turned around to open the door. But before heading out, he asked, "Are you okay?"

"Yea, I'm good." *With yo fine ass.* I looked him up and down and no sooner than my eyes made it back up to the top of his head, my panties were moist.

"You sure? What you up to?" Riq asked, stalling a little, closing the door slightly.

"Not shit. Just bored and 'bout to order some food and watch a movie." *I can really use some company but I told myself I wasn't going to do this anymore.*

Tariq turned to face me and the throbbing started up again. I dared not to look him in his face. I knew that once our souls connected through our eyes, I could no longer stand a chance. I had been doing so good lately by staying away from Tariq and doing the right thing.

"Why you acting like you don't miss a nigga? Mo, I know you miss me. You can't even look me in the face. You in here drinking and shit and the only time you drink like that is when you mad. I know you ain't happy being here alone. If you were mine, do you think I would leave you like this by yourself? Plus, you looking all sexy and shit. When you gon' realize that nigga ain't for you?"

I instantly turned away before allowing the tears to fall from my face. *"Maybe Tariq is right. I shouldn't be here like this,"* I thought.

Tariq walked up toward me and grabbed my waist, pulling me in close to him. His cologne consumed me, making me even wetter.

"Aye, look, let me just chill with you. It'll make me feel better. I don't like you here alone like this."

Before I could answer, Tariq kissed me passionately, backing me up against the couch, making me take a seat. I sat back and watched him as he took off his jacket and hat and kneeled down to get on his knees. I could no longer fight it, I needed some bad. I let the tears roll down my face as Tariq lifted up my thin, silk robe to take my panties off.

"Lord knows I need this. Please, Lord, forgive me."

"Damn, baby girl, you wet as fuck. Seem like you been missing daddy." Tariq slowly stuck one finger in and out of my pussy.

I rolled my eyes, while watching Tariq kiss all over my inner thighs as he slowly massaged my insides.

"You know it, big daddy." I agreed, pretending that his comment was true.

The fact of the matter was Tariq's dick was big but he didn't know how to use it to its full potential. He always came as soon as he got inside of me, and because I knew this, I always made him eat my pussy first. Being sure to get mines before he took his. Plus, I just wanted to cum. I wasn't concerned about pleasing him this time.

He lacked in the sex department but he made up for it when he gave head. The closer he got to the center of my preciousness, the closer the chills came to rushing over my body. "*Damn, nigga, stop playing with it,*" I thought. "*I'm 'bout to nut in this nigga's mouth and make him leave.*"

I was more than ready for it and Riq was taking too long. Suddenly, he entered my pussy with his tongue, sucking in and out and slurping every bit of wetness there was.

"Uhhhhh, Riiiiqq!" I moaned, while trying to resist him.

Riq stopped for a split second.

"There you go with that running shit." he spat with attitude while looking up at me and grabbing my thighs to hold me down. "Stop running, girl, and take this shit," he demanded before going back to feast on my pussy.

He licked back and forth on the tip of my clitoris slowly. As I began to jerk, I could feel my juices run from my pussy down to my ass cheeks.

"Right there, Riq. Right there. Don't stop. Ummmmmm, please don't stop." I placed my hand on top of his head being sure to push it down as I rocked my ass back and forth, fucking his face. Showering him with all of my sweet wetness, I belted, "Ooooooooouuu, I'm cumming." I laid there jerking while Riq kept sucking and sucking, being sure to get every drop. I blessed his face over and over again.

I was cumming so much I began to tense up.

"Just relax, Mo. Just relax and let it out. You know I love when you cum for me."

I loved cumming for Tariq just as much as he loved making me cum, but I never told him.

I laid there shaking from the intense nut that I just had as Riq went to use the restroom.

"He can't stay the night here," I thought.

Devin usually called at 7:30 on his way to work each morning and I had to make sure I answered his call. "I know he gon have a fit as soon as I tell this nigga he gotta go." I got up and quickly gathered his clothes, being sure he didn't leave or drop anything before he returned from the restroom. I heard the toilet flushing and waited to hear Tariq cut on the water to wash his hands, letting me know that time was running out. I couldn't find my panties and decided to slip my robe on without them. I picked up his shirt and hat.

"Oh, so you just gon put me out?" Tariq was standing at the door butt naked with his dick standing at attention. He was so hard I wasn't sure if I should freeze and put my hands up or drop down to my knees and give him face time immediately.

"Why do he keep doing this to me?" I thought to myself. I opened my mouth to answer Tariq but nothing came out. I was stuck. Every time I went to speak, my mouth would open and close again. I felt as though his beautiful, black, long, thick dick had me mesmerized and he knew it. Suddenly, Riq's phone rang startling me out of my trance. "You know you got to go, Tariq. Devin gon be calling in the morning," I said as I looked over to his jacket at his ringing cell phone.

Riq didn't budge or move. Refusing to take his eyes off of me, he just let the phone ring and ring.

"So what, tell that nigga you with me."

"You know I can't do that Riq. I'm with Devin"

"Then why the hell you got me here, Mo? Answer that shit for Me. Devin being my brother didn't mean shit to you when you were squirting on my face a second ago. Did it?"

A part of me was ashamed for betraying Devin, but the other part of me needed him in my life and he wasn't there. No matter how much I tried to stay away from Tariq, I couldn't. Everything about him reminded me of Devin. He had the same dark chocolate skin, very fit muscular body, and the size of their dicks was amazing. They were identical for God's sake, and because he wasn't here like I needed him to be, I went to the closest thing to him, his twin brother

"See, that's why I can't fuck with you. Every time, it never fails, you start talking crazy and shit." Riq and I had been messing for a year now. We both agreed that we would keep each other satisfied with no strings attached, but the more dealings we had, the more feelings came. So I had to back away. I would be lying if I said I hadn't caught any feelings myself. The only difference was I was better at not showing them.

"You know what, Mo, you're right. I'm wrong. Maybe we shouldn't continue to do this anymore. Just come get the rest of your shit from my crib tomorrow, and let this be it"

Tariq grabbed his clothes, and then grabbed his jacket off the chair, putting it on. Quickly, he picked up his phone, looked at it for a min, and then put the phone back into his pocket

I felt bad for using Tariq because a part of me wished I could give him more of me, but I couldn't. I belonged to another man. Tariq turned to go out the door. He grabbed the handle to let himself out, and just as he opened the door, I noticed the clippers sitting on the stand by the door.

"Tariq, you forgetting something."

"Oh yea, I was looking for those."

As I handed him the clippers, silence filled the air until Tariq broke it.

"Can I ask you one thing?"

Knowing exactly what was about to come next, I said, "Sure, what's up?"

"What's so different? Why him?"

I knew Tariq loved me, and in fact, I loved him too. But he wanted something from me that I couldn't give, something that I wasn't willing to give, which was all of me in exchange for him.

"Because he's my husband."

DEVIN

As Janell laid on my chest while I hit my blunt, I thought about the day I first laid eyes on her. Shorty was bad as fuck from the top of her head to the bottom of her feet. I had been eyeing her ever since Monae had thrown a wine tasting party at the house last August. I asked myself, *"Who is she?"*

Her complexion was the color of honey. And every time she smiled or giggled, it made her Chinese eyes look even more chinky. The Marilyn Monroe piercing was sexy above her big juicy lips and I found myself daydreaming about what it would feel like to get my dick sucked by her. I kept telling myself the whole night, "*I'm gon get that ass.*" The body was shaped so perfectly beautiful. Her waist was small and thin and her ass was phat and firm and cuved at the bottom like an onion. I couldn't seem to take my eyes off of her. Her caramel complexion glowed from the minute she walked in. The eye contact we made told me she wanted me just as bad as I wanted her. We flirted the whole night with our eyes, being sure not to let everyone in on our hidden connection.

"Dang, nigga, pass the blunt."

"Oh, my bad, bae. My bad." I had forgotten that quick that Janelle was laying on me.

"What are you over there thinking about anyway?" Janelle asked as she tried to grip the ends of the blunt with her fingertips.

"I'm over here thinking 'bout yo ass. A nigga was happy as fuck when you hit me up on Facebook. I didn't know how I was gon get in touch with you without Monae knowing, but you had been on my mind every day since."

"You still be thinking 'bout that? Janelle asked, giggling. "That's been over a year now, babe," She said smiling as she got up to straddle me.

"I know. I know," I replied, staring Janelle in her face, trying not to smile to hard. While I watched her hit the blunt repeatedly, I thought it was cute to see her smoke a blunt, considering that she was nothing like Monae. She acted like a geek, really shy, and portrayed the good girl role. But she was freakier than any women I knew. By just looking at her you would have never assumed.

"Speaking of our anniversary is coming up really soon. I was thinking maybe we should fly to Miami for a weekend," she suggested while coughing and trying to pass the blunt back to me.

I wasn't sure about doing the whole Miami trip thing with Janelle. *"I got to let her go soon,"* I thought, considering any free time I had from work I spent with Monae. But Janelle didn't know that. I told her that me and Monae had split up after moving to DC because the long-distance relationship was becoming too stressful for her. But the truth of it all was that I was still happily married and had no intentions of leaving Monae. I went home every weekend to see her and Janelle came to DC every other week during the week days to stay with me. She was the CEO for a multimillion dollar business and did most of her work from home so that allowed her to pick up and go, getting her job done anywhere there was internet. *"I know I gotta break things off with Janelle soon."*

"Bae, I'm not sure about a Miami trip right now," I said, taking the blunt from her and hitting it one more time before putting it out. "But don't you worry about that, let me handle the plans," I continued, raising up on my elbows and kissing her seductively."

Janelle returned the kiss. Sucking on her bottom lip, I took my time to ease my tongue in her mouth, slowly flipping her over underneath me. I pulled her shirt over her head, going for her tittes. Cupping both breasts in my hand, I caressed them one by one. Giving the right one my full attention first, sucking on the nipple gently.

"I missed you" she spoke so softly.

"I missed you too, bae," I replied, playfully going to her left tittie to give it the same amount of affection.

I slowly made my way down her stomach as I placed kisses all over her body. Janelle's body scent was like a fresh flower, lightly scented and very addictive. I couldn't wait to smell her pussy. My dick swole inside my sweat pants as I thought about how good Janelle's pussy was.

"Take them thangs off," I demanded while tugging at her black thongs with the word pink written on them in bold white letters.

While she came out of her panties, I removed my gray sweats quickly. "*I'm 'bout to fuck the shit out of her,*" I thought as I watched her nude body. Returning back to the bed, I climbed on top of her, spreading her legs wide. Slowly rubbing on her thighs, I began to kiss the lips of her pussy as if I was kissing her face, making her wetter than an otter's pocket. The smell of water graced the tip of my nose as her precum greased my face.

"You ready for me bae?" I asked.

"Yes," she answered.

"Well turn over for me then."

Janelle did as instructed, getting on her knees in the doggy style position. I pulled her all the way to me so that her feet were hanging off the edge of the bed. I stood behind her, taking the palm of my hands and placing them on her ass cheeks, being sure to extend my thumbs to the middle of her asshole to give her a long massage. I could sense that Janelle was a little tense and I wanted her to relax. After massaging her with my fingers, I separated her ass cheeks as far as I could and jumped right in with my tongue, making my tongue flat to lick her asshole up and down, and then around, slowly repeating my lick.

"Umm, bae, what are you doing?" Janelle asked in a low sexy tone while looking back at me.

"Shhhhhh, don't move."

I made my tongue pointy to penetrate her asshole. Then I slowly reached around the front to finger her pussy.

"Ooooohhhhhhh," Janelle whined.

"You like this shit, don't you?"

"I loovvee iiit." Janelle was barely able to talk.

I knew the type of shit I was doing would make Janelle fall in love with a nigga, but for some reason, I felt like it was too late for that. Over and over, I had practiced how I was gonna break shit off with her, but I couldn't. Every time I wanted to see Monae and couldn't, I called Janelle. I knew I was playing a dangerous game by fucking my wife's boss. I was in way too deep and it was too late to fall back now. I could only imagine how bad things would end if I did. The thought of her blackmailing me or firing Monae from her job made me want to fuck her more. I removed my finger from inside her pussy and noticed how soaked it was. I grabbed my dick and rubbed her juices on my stiff brick. Then I suddenly entered her from the back.

"Aaaahhhh!" she screamed out.

I began going in and out at an easy pace, filling her up with all of my seven inches.

"This shit so good. I couldn't wait to get inside of you."

Holding her thighs as I slid in and out, I realized that Janelle was trying to throw it back faster, making her ass slap faster and faster against me. Her asshole was smacking, gushing, and making slurping noises, which was making me even harder, on top of her moans.

"Ho-ld up," I managed to get out while trying to slow down my stroke to stop myself from nutting.

"No, bae, I'm 'bout to cum."

"Shit!" I could feel the buildup come as my eyes rolled to the back of my head.

"Yesss, go deeper, Devin, deeper," Janelle yelled out to me.

"Errrrrr deeper, huh?" I asked while I used her hips to guide me in and out as hard and fast as I could. We were in competition, putting in work, sexually fighting to see who would get their nut first.

"Yasssss! Yassss! Yaaaass."

"Well, then cum on my dick."

Our breathing was heavy on one accord as our moans made a sexy tone. The bed was squeaking and my knees had gotten weak right at my peak.

We had both reached our climax at the same time.

"Oh! Oh! Oh1" I stuttered, while jerking inside of Janelle.

"Uhhhhhhhhhhhh, I'm cumming on daddy's dick."

I could feel Janelle gushing out. It felt like I was draining inside of her.

"Ahhhh! You cumming on daddy's dick?

"Yaasss!"

"Well, cum on that shit, then."

The End

Fuck Fest Extravaganza
By MisChievous

Chapter 1

Cameron White is the name, everyone calls me Cam. I'm a thirty-year-old nurse at *Northwestern Hospital* in Chicago, Illinois. I graduated from *Northern University* with honors, earning my nursing degree. My life is everything that I want it to be, except for the fact that I'm single as fuck. Living my life like an old ass woman was not in my plans. All I do is work, eat, shit, and sleep. I have to spice up my life, and I need to do it now.

I hit the button on my alarm, rolled out of bed, and walked past the full-length mirror, all I saw was ass. "*Damn, your ass fat, bitch*!" I laughed to myself. Standing five feet seven inches, one hundred fifty-four pounds, light skin, high cheekbones, and pouty lips. All of my weight is in my ass, that's the first thing everyone see when looking at me from behind. My lips is the first thing that's noticed when they're looking in my face. I hate it so much. I can suck the skin off a dick but I don't need to be reminded of the shit.

I walked to the closet and skimmed through the clothes, trying to decided what I wanted to wear for the day. I chose grey joggers, grey long sleeved pink belly top, and pulled my grey and white Air Force 1s out the box. I can dress down and I'm still sexy as hell.

I made my way to the bathroom and took care of my hygiene. Stepping in the shower, I let the hot water glide over my body, and it felt so good. I rubbed my hands across my breasts, and felt a tingling sensation starting in my stomach. I lifted my right nipple to my mouth. I sucked and bit down on it while my other hand caressed my love box. Slipping two fingers in to my slippery hole, I gasped.

"Mmmmm," I moaned while my tongue flicked my nipple faster.

My pussy was so hot at the moment, I had to put the fire out. I knew for a fact that the sensation was not gonna be enough. Fucking myself with damn near my entire hand, I finally threw my head back and came hard. "Aaaahhhhh shit!" I cried out.

After I caught my breath and came down from my orgasm, I washed my body with my strawberry mango body wash, from head to toe. With my eyes closed, I reached for my face towel to wash my face. I hated when females use the same towel to wash their ass and their face. That shit is disgusting. I grabbed my plush towel and stepped out of the shower. I ran my fingers through my hair, checking out my Locs in the mirror. Yeah, they were still looking fresh. I applied oil to my hair, and a light coat of makeup. Yep, it was time to get dressed. I put on my clothes, grabbed my keys and Burberry shades, and was out the door.

I pushed the gas pedal until the speedometer hit fifty, merging onto Lake Shore Drive towards the Pancake House in Hyde Park. My mind started wandering to the last time my body had been touched. It had been so long that honestly, I couldn't remember. Other than self-pleasure, my shit been dry. It was time for me to figure out how I was gonna be spontaneous and get my pussy worked on.

I hit the alarm on my 2017 Jeep Cherokee and entered the restaurant. I loved coming to this place because the breakfast was to die for.

"Welcome to the Original Pancake House, are you dining alone today?" the hostess asked.

"Thank you, and yes, I am."

"Alright, follow me. Do you prefer a booth or table?"

"A table by the window will be fine thanks."

After being seated, my phone rang in my purse. I pulled it out and saw that it was my ex. I rolled my eyes and answered.

"Hello," I spoke with attitude.

"Hello, stranger, how are you? Why haven't I heard from you?" Julian asked.

Julian was my ex. I didn't know why his ass was always on my phone when he was the one that ended our relationship. You would've thought that if he wanted out, he would've stayed the fuck out. But that wasn't the case at all. Every time I turned around, he was dialing my damn phone. I didn't have time for that shit right now.

"Julian, why do you constantly call me? I'm so confused. You wanted to move on with the next bitch, but you seem to always bother me. What is it? The bitch ain't so appealing after all, huh?" I laughed.

"I miss u, Cam-"

"I'm not even trying to hear that, Julian. What I want is for you to continue to do you, because I'm doing me. There is no way possible I'm about to entertain this nonsense with you today. You made your bed, now lie in it!" I said, tapping the button to end the call.

He continued to call and I ignored him every time. The waitress came over, took my order, and brought me a glass of water and a glass of orange juice. Just thinking about the French toast, scrambled eggs with cheese, grits, turkey bacon, and a bowl of fruit, my stomach growled. I decided to finish up *Thugs Cry* by *Ca$h* on my Kindle while I waited.

My food finally arrived, and I was ready to tear into it. I bit into a forkful of eggs and was in heaven, damn near cummin' from the taste on my tongue. Out of the corner of my eye, I saw this fine ass man staring at me with so much lust in his eyes. I grabbed a strawberry and sensually raised it to my lips, savoring the taste with my eyes closed. I opened my eyes, looked over to my left, and smiled.

"*I can have some fun with his ass,*" I giggled.

He had the prettiest golden brown eyes I had seen in a very long time. Those pink ass lips made my kitty tingle with all the nasty thoughts that was in my head. I licked my lips, winked my eye, and then blew him a kiss. *When did I get so damn bold?* I had never initiated anything with a guy. *I guess it's time to show out*, I said to myself. I stood up, collected my shit, and walked over to Mr. Handsome's table.

"Is this seat taken?" I asked seductively.

"It is now, beautiful. Have a seat," he replied with this husky baritone.

Once situated, I started eating my food, which was cold now, waiting on him to say something. When he didn't, I initiated the conversation, since the cat had his tongue.

"I'm Cam. I thought I would come over since you were staring a hole in my face," I said while smiling.

"Nice to meet you, Cam. I'm sorry about that. But you are so beautiful. My name is Micah, by the way," he said shyly.

Micah had beautiful dimples that got deeper the more he smiled. His goatee was trimmed to perfection as well. I zoned out, thinking about what that mouth do. My pussy was throbbing. Smiling and licking my lips, his voice brought me out of my trance.

"Penny for your thoughts?" he asked while smiling at me.

I took a small sip of my orange juice and boldly stated, "I was just thinking about how good your lips would feel on my body."

A surprised look washed across his face, but he recovered smoothly. "Wanna find out?" he chuckled.

Mustering up the nerve to call his bluff, I continued to drink my OJ. "Yeah, let's find out," I smirked.

I grabbed my wallet to pay for my breakfast that I barely touched. He reached out and touched my hand, shaking his head. "I got it, beautiful," he insisted. I didn't argue with him at all. I know how to let a man be a gentleman.

Leaving the restaurant, I felt jittery because I had never done anything like this before. But I needed to fuck badly and Micah was about to be a great candidate. This man gave grey sweatpants a new meaning. When I say that I saw the imprint of his dick precisely, almost had me drooling prematurely.

I couldn't keep my eyes off of it at all.

"Do you like what you see?" he asked arrogantly.

"I sure do," I said seductively.

I gently held his hand and led him to the back of the restaurant. It was pretty secluded out there, and I was feeling kind of adventurous at that point. There was no time for trying to spend money for a room, what's that? He followed with no hesitation. With my back on the wall, Micah stood in front of me with all of the muscles on his six foot three inch frame, looking like a caramel Twix bar.

"Are you sure you wanna do this?" he asked softly.

"I'm positive," I said, biting my lip.

Micah ran his hands up and down my sides, trailing my dolphin tattoo that was on my rib cage. He bent down, planting kisses along my neck, while his hands massaged my breast. Realizing that I didn't have on a bra, he tweaked my nipples until they protruded through my shirt. He held my breast in his hand, brought his mouth down to my nipple, and suckled like a baby nursing for the first time. My clit was swollen, my legs were shaking. In my head, I was like, *I know this man is not about to make me cum by sucking on my titties.*

"Mmmmmmmmm," I moaned lowly.

He attacked my breasts ferociously with his mouth. He was handling all of my 36Cs with no assistance at all. Bringing both of his hands to my ass, he squeezed and molded both cheeks like he was a sculptor or some shit. I'm not gonna lie, it felt good as hell. He eased his hands all the way into my pants, his fingers found my mound, and the way he was caressing my clit, I felt like I was melting. I was on the brink of cumming at that precise moment.

"Damn, baby, I'm about to cum," I gasped, grabbing the back of his head.

"Let that shit go then! What the fuck you announcing it for?" he barked.

Caressing my slit, Micah slipped two fingers in to my wet hole. I started fucking his fingers like it was his dick. He snaked a third finger in and my breath caught in my throat. I felt the wetness of my nectar running down my thighs, so I knew his hand was soaked.

"Damn, this pussy wet as fuck, ma," he groaned while biting my ear.

He yanked my joggers down with his free hand, and lifted me high on the wall. My kitty was all in his face. He closed his eyes and sniffed my snatch long and hard.

"This muthafucka smell good, too. Let me find out what she taste like," he mumbled.

Placing my legs on his shoulders, he was putting those muscles to the test, and he passed with flying colors. Lifting me like I was light as a feather, he planted his mouth on my clit with no hesitation. The feeling of his lips sent electrifying currents shooting up my spine.

"Oh shit! Eat it, baby, yes!" I moaned.

Eyes rolling in my head like marbles, I rocked my hips back and forth on his face, until I was lightheaded. He curled his tongue in my tunnel, it was stiff and long. I was bouncing on it like it was a mini dick. The feeling was damn near paralyzing.

"Yes, yes, yes, I'm cumming! Fucccckkkkkk!" I screamed, squirting everywhere and muffling the sound with my fist.

"Damn, babygirl, I love that shit," Micah said seductively while wiping his mouth.

Not giving me a chance to recuperate, he placed me down on the ground and turned me towards the wall. I heard the condom being ripped open. I glanced over my shoulder and saw his dick standing at attention like a baseball bat. In my mind, I was screaming, *"Oh hell naw!"*

But that was what the fuck I wanted and I was about to take one for the team. I was not running from that shit.

He stepped up behind me slowly, moving my Locs and kissing me on the back of my neck. He eased in my sweet spot and stroked slowly. That man was really making love to me in the back of a damn restaurant! I was not complaining because he was rocking my pussy. I guessed he sensed that my mind was wandering because he started hitting me hard as fuck.

"Ummmmph, sssssssss, yes!" I cried out, running from his dick.

"What you runnin' fo? This what you wanted, right? Take this dick like I know you can," he demanded.

"Ooooooouu! Shit yes!"

Micah kept his stroke coming, faster and harder, hitting every organ in my body. He reached around, rubbing my clit as he fucked me with no mercy at all. My clit harden and I knew I was about to cum like a river. Grunting in my ear with every stroke he took, that man turned into a sexual beast.

"Yes! Fuck me, Micah! Fuck me harder!" I purred, throwing my ass back on him, meeting him stroke for stroke.

"Yeah, fuck this dick, baby! Take. This. Nut!"

"Uh, uh, uh, yes!" I screamed while he smacked my ass, making me squirt everywhere.

All that could be heard was grunts and moans at that point. Micah continue to pound my pussy, vigorously. I felt like I was high as hell. I hadn't been sexed like that in... Never! He was fucking me so good my eyes were rolling to the back of my head. Sensing that Micah was about to cum, my own orgasm was nearing. My silky walls closed in around his hard dick, I bounced back on it and wasn't letting up. I was gonna get one more out of that run.

"Damn, you gripping this dick, girl! You got some good as pussy. Grrrrrr shit, ma!" he growled.

"Don't stop! I'm almost there, Micah, I'm almost there!" I cried.

"Cum with me, Cam!" Micah groaned while pumping faster.

We both exploded at the same time. It was like time stood still. That was the best orgasm I'd ever had!

Micah looked at me with a sensual look that made my pussy thump with every breath I took. I reached for my purse, pulled out the wet wipes that I keep with me, handed some to him, and cleaned myself. Once I fixed my clothes, I looked at Micah and said, "Thanks," and walked away.

Chapter 2

I had never done anything like the shit I did yesterday. A part of me just felt ashamed, but my inner sex goddess was proud of herself. Don't get me wrong, the way Micah fucked me was indescribable. I went home and slept for the rest of the day with a smile on my face.

Once I awoke, I was horny as hell and needed another fix. I was kind of scared of the spontaneous shit, but I was excited at the same damn time. Who knew what I would get myself into today, I couldn't wait to find out.

My body was aching for great reasons, but I couldn't shake the fact that I had a craving to fuck. Many people craved food, my sex crazed ass was craving sex. After taking care of my hygiene, I dressed and left the house. With no destination in mind, I jumped in my Jeep and just started to drive.

Thinking about my aching muscles, I decided to go get a massage at *Sensual Seductions*. I hadn't been to this massage parlor in a while, but my body needed a good rub down. I hated that it was all the way in Hinsdale, but it was worth it. Traffic was not too bad, so I would be alright.

It was too quiet, so turned on Sirius radio, *Trey Songz 1x1* blared through the speakers.

Now it's 3am, I'm back for more, yea/ just two of us/ show me what I'm waiting for/ one by one, one by one, o-one.

I loved that song, had me kind of beating myself up for not getting Micah's number for another round. One time wasn't enough for me, I needed some more. Oh well, it was on to the next one.

Getting through the traffic was a breeze. I pulled up to the parlor, grabbed my purse, and made my way inside. This place was always so relaxing and inviting. You could get lost within yourself from the atmosphere alone. Yeah, I was about to get the tension out of my body.

"May I help you?" the receptionist asked.

"Yes, I would like to get a ninety minute Swedish massage," I replied.

The primary goal of a Swedish massage technique was to relax the body, decrease muscle toxins, and improve flexibility while easing tension. Shit that was what the fuck I needed right then. The extracurricular activity I indulged in yesterday had my shit in knots.

"Aaah, that's one of the best massages that we have. Great choice, follow me," she said, leading me to a room in the back.

"Your masseuse will be Lexi today. You can undress, hang your belongings in the closet, drape the towel over your body, and relax. Lexi will be in shortly," she explained.

"Thank you so much," I politely responded.

Disrobing, I hung my clothes in the closet, put my earbuds in my ear, and relaxed. Not realizing that someone entered the room, I felt a tap on my shoulder. Removing the earbuds, I looked up to see who was touching me. What I saw standing before me took my breath away. I had never been attracted to a woman, ever, but that bitch was gorgeous.

She had to me Dominican or something. Her hair was jet black and curly as hell, framing her blemish free face perfectly, lips full and succulent, eyes the greyest I'd ever seen on a human, titties sittin' right, small waist, and a big dumb ass! She had on some yoga type pants, pussy looking like she had a fist in the front of them muthafuckas. I couldn't believe that my mouth was watering because of this chic.

Lexi snapped me out of my trance, she spoke with an accent that was so soft and sensual.

"Hi, I'm Lexi, I'll be your masseuse for the day. Do you have any questions?"

I couldn't even speak, I just shook my head no. All I knew was that my mind was in the gutta like a muthafucka. I was trying to figure out how I was about to have this fine ass bitch sitting on my face. "*Did I just say that shit to myself? I'm surprising myself more and more as the time goes by,"* I said in my mind while shaking my head.

Lexi was getting all of her supplies together while I watched her ass bounce around like jelly. I wanted her badly, my treasure box was pulsating like crazy. Don't ask because I don't know, I was clueless at that point. That thang had a mind of its own.

She turned the lights down, walked over to a table, and lit a couple of candles. She pressed the play button on her phone and *Ro James' Permission* filled the room.

With your permission/ I just wanna spend a little time with you, ooh/ With your permission/ Tonight I wanna be a little me on you, oh yeah/With your permission/ I wanna spend the night sippin' on you/ You know what I'm talking about baby, yeah
Now it's time for you to show me what it's hitting for/ Sip a little jack, maybe blow a little dro/ Love you from behind but I hate to see you go

She walked towards me with a bottle of almond oil in her hand and a sensual smile on her face. Squirting a small amount into the palm of her hands, she started to rub my shoulders with long strokes. My eyes closed instantly. It felt so good. Her hands were soft and she was applying pressure and rotating her fingers slowly. She eased up off my shoulders, I didn't feel her for a quick minute.

But then her hands were on my neck, getting the kinks out.

"Mmmmmmmm, yeah, just like that," I groaned.

My pussy was wet as hell because all I saw behind my eyelids was her pussy print. I was feenin' for this chic, for real. Her hands were kneading the small of my back, then she removed the towel and started kneading my ass cheeks. I almost came instantly.

"Mmmmmmmm," I moaned.

"You like that?" she asked.

"Yes I do," I answered.

"So that means you like this as well. Huh?" she asked as she rubbed my pussy from the back.

Realizing that she put *Permission* on repeat, she was asking me for the green light. Hell Yeah! It's on!

"Mmmmmmhmmmm," I moaned.

I snaked my ass up so she could really play with my cookies. She parted my ass and stuck her tongue in my ass. That shit felt good as hell. I had never been with a woman, but you only live once. Throwing my ass back on her tongue, I was moaning loudly. It felt like she was penetrating my soul with her every stroke. I looked over my shoulder and realized that this freaky bitch was butt ass naked. Yeah, she knew I was down when I fucked her with my eyes from the jump. My body was hotter than fish grease. I was about to get turned out and I was about to love every bit of it.

She removed her tongue from my ass, and went in head first into my love box. She was eating my twat like she never wanted to come up for air.

"Oh shit, girl, eat that shit!" I purred.

I didn't want her to ease up off my clit for nothing. She applied pressure with her tongue like a pro. I felt her tongue curled upward, entering my hole like she was scooping ice cream out of a bowl. Arching my back, I held onto the sheet with all my might. I damn near cried out because she had my spine rigid as hell. Slipping her index and middle finger into my pussy, she clamped down on my clit with her lips, hard. She was trying to suck my breath out of me, and it was working. Reaching back, I opened my ass cheeks so she could really get in there and quench her thirst.

"Damn, yes! I'm cummmmin'!" I screamed.

She smacked my ass hard as hell and my body shook on contact. I came so hard I squirted all in her mouth and she didn't let a drop fall. She slurped up every ounce. She backed off my kitty while licking her lips and turned me over on my back. Rubbing her fingertips up and down my slit, pinching and blowing on my clit. She pulled up a chair and dove back in.

"Sabes tan bien," (You taste so good), Lexi said sensually in Spanish.

That shit made my nipples hard when I heard it. I didn't know what the fuck she said but it was hot as hell. She was doing figure eights in my snatch so fast that my legs were getting weak with each stroke. Throwing my legs behind my head, she went in. Flicking her tongue up and down, around, back and forth, the friction was unbearable.

"Oooooooouuu! Shit, shit, shit! Damn, what the fuck are you doing to me?" I cried.

This bitch was eating my pussy better than any nigga I'd ever been with. And she knew that shit, too. She started humming on my clit like she was singing a song. The vibration was electrical and sharp. I felt all types of tingling sensations in my toes. Her head game was the truth.

Lexi rose from the chair, running her hands gently up my leg. She climbed on top of the table with me. Mounting my body, she started grinding her pussy against mine.

"Oh shit! What the fuck?" I exclaimed.

"Eres tan hermosa cuando estás al borde de la explosion," (you are so beautiful when you are on the brink of exploding), she smiled sexily.

I'd seen this shit in porn but never thought it would feel good like this. My clit was sticking out like a baby dick, and smacking against her. I was about to blow a gasket. She started moving back and forth faster, my stomach muscles were tightening up fast. My release was building up at a rapid pace, one final stroke and I exploded.

"Oh emmmmm geeee!" I yelled.

"¡Sí, mamá! Deja que esa mierda se vaya!" (Yes, mama! Let that shit go!), she exclaimed.

She caressed my breasts, then she smiled down at me. "Te sientes tan bien, me encantan los sonidos que haces cuando sueltas." (You feel so good. I love the sounds you make when you release.)

"What did u say? It sounds so beautiful," I asked.

She repeated what she said in English, had my ass blushing and shit. Lexi climbed off of the table and told me where the showers were. I showered and put my clothes on. When I got back to the room, Lexi was nowhere in sight. But there was a note on the table that read:

You taste so good, baby. Thanks for letting me make you feel like you're walking on clouds. Whenever you need to release some pressure, you know where to cum. This one's on me, enjoy the rest of your day beautiful. Besos (kisses), Lexi

Chapter 3

I couldn't understand where all of the sexual desire was coming from. I shocked myself with all of the shit that I had been doing. Driving from the spa, I was all in my feelings trying to determine if what happened means I like women. I was not gonna think about it too much because I enjoyed every bit of it. I really didn't care what the fuck anyone had to say about it.

My truck needs a good washing. I think I will head to the car wash. Pulling up to Pierre's, a well-known car wash where all the fine niggas got their cars washed, I went inside to get the ultimate wash for my baby. She needed the best that they provided.

My phone chimed, indicating that I had a message on Facebook. Paying too much attention to my phone and walking, I ran right into something hard. Juggling my phone and catching it before it hit the ground, I looked up and saw a fine nigga standing before me.

When I say fine, this man stood about six feet, two hundred pounds, milk chocolate complexion, dreads hanging down his back, twisted in designs. His eyes were like cat eyes, light brown, grey, and a tint of green, and almond shaped, looking like he could hypnotize my ass with one look.

"Damn, ma, you ok? My fault, I wasn't paying attention," he said apologetically.

"It's ok, I wasn't looking where I was going either. So I guess we were both in the wrong," I shot back, trying to walk around him.

He grabbed me by my arm. I looked down at his hand, and he let me go. Holding his hands up in a surrender motion, he tried to explain, "My bad, ma, I shouldn't have touched you at all. I just want to get to know you."

"I'm not trying to get to know anyone at this time. I just want to have fun. Now if you want to do that, then let's make it happen," I said without hesitation.

"What's your definition of fun, ma? That statement can go many ways, you know," he said with a smirk.

"Whatever you come up with, I'm with it. But I have to get my car washed real quick."

"I got you. Only the best for a beauty such as yourself," he said, walking into the office.

When he emerged after paying, he walked with me to my car. Opening my passenger door, he motioned for me to get in.

With a raised eyebrow and my hand on my hip, I had to ask, "Why are you directing me to the passenger seat of *my* car?"

"Just get your cute ass in the car, ma," he said cockily.

To be honest, that shit turned me on. I got my ass in the car because I needed to know what he had up his sleeve. He held his hand out for my keys and I gave them to him. He walked to the driver side and got in. Starting up the car, he pulled up to pull into the wash. Mr. Mystery Man turned on the radio and *Chris Brown's Back to Sleep* blared loudly.

Just let me rock/fuck you back to sleep, girl/ oh, don't say a word, no/ girl don't you talk, oh yeah/ just hold on tight to me, girl/ fuck you back to sleep, girl, rock you back

He turned his head looking at me, licking his lips like *LL Cool J.* My pussy twerked all on its own, probably just as excited as me about what that mouth do. Mr. Mystery pulled into the car wash and put the car in neutral. Usually, the wash would start right away, but today it didn't.

"Why isn't the wash starting?" I asked him.

"I paid for the Ultimate extended wash. Now bring your sexy ass over here," he said seductively.

I moved sensually toward him, thinking about what I wanted to do to him. It was obvious that Mr. Mystery wanted to fuck, and so did I. Shit, I was still trying to find out where all of this was coming from, but the inner nasty bitch within myself was coaxing me to shut the fuck up and do it. I snatched a gold wrapper from the middle console, opened it, and placed it in my mouth.

Never taking my eyes off of him, I unbuckled his pants and let his long muscle fall out. His dick was about eight and a half inches, and thick as hell. Veins were popping in every direction, letting me know that he was ready. I wrapped my hand around his pipe, stroking it up and down while rotating my hand.

Mr. Mystery let out a low moan, looking me straight in my face. “Let me see what that mouth do, ma.”

Without second guessing my actions, I lowered my head and applied the condom with my mouth. Taking his dick in all the way to the base. With my hands mounted on his thigh, I worked his pipe with no hands. I swallowed that muthafucka while Mr. Mystery gripped the back of my head.

“Damn, ma! Suck that dick, baby! Get all that dick! Ahhhhhh yes, ma! Just like that!” he moaned lowly.

I had never heard a man that damn verbal during sex. I just wanted him to shut the fuck up and take this shit. I guess he read my mind because when I picked up the pace and started jerking his dick with both hands, he bossed the fuck up.

“I want to feel nothing but throat, no gagging, and no muthafuckin’ hands! Just like that!”

I almost came off those words alone. He grabbed a handful of my hair and started fucking my mouth vigorously and I was lovin it! He wasn’t letting up at all. Twirling my tongue around the head of his dick, I sucked it hard as hell, making a popping sound. His eyes were rolling in the back of his head. Moaning on his dick, I was on the brink of cummin'.

Mr. Mystery wasn't ready to cum just yet. He laid the seat down and moved it back as far as it would go.

"Come out them muthafuckin' pants and climb on my face. I know that pussy is sweet and juicy. I just want to taste it for myself."

I loved the way he demanded shit around this bitch. *That's right, nigga, take charge.* I took off my pants at the precise time that the wash started up. The sound of the music and the machines in the wash set the mood. Mounting his face, Mr. Mystery took hold of my thighs and dived right in.

"Mmmmm, yeah! Right there!" I screamed.

My pussy was leaking in no time. The way he was moving his tongue, I thought there was a snake between my legs. Rocking my hips back and forth, back and forth, I was building the momentum to get the nut that I was seeking, squeezing my breasts and pinching my nipples. Mr. Mystery sucked my clit long and hard, and soon after he was wearing my nectar as aftershave.

He held me by my waist and reversed the position. We were halfway through the wash at this time, but we didn't seem to give a damn. He kissed me from my neck, down to my breasts, giving both of them equal attention. Kneading my breasts while suckling was a wonderful feeling. Without using any hands, he eased all of that dick in to my cookie jar.

"Aaahhhhhh! Sssssss!" I moaned.

"Oh shit, this pussy is good!" he yelled, pumping my shit hard.

Mr. Mystery was punishing my kitty and he didn't even have beef with her. With his face contorted into this ugly grimace, he was damn near drooling from being all in this gushy good-good.

"Damn, ma, yeah! Squeeze this dick just like that! Ooooooh, ooooh, ooooh!" he moaned loudly while getting his *R Kelly* on.

He lifted my legs to my head and held me there while he beat my pussy up so good! I couldn't formulate one word, but I turned into the sound effect queen.

"Aaaahhhhh! Oooooooouuu! Mmmmmmmmm! Sssssssss! Uuuummm!"

This man was hitting every part of my ovaries, and there was nothing I could do about it. He had me in a pretzel-like position and all he was delivering was hard shots, nonstop. The squishy sound that my love box was making matched the sounds of the wash at the moment. We were nearing the end of the wash and we were still going full throttle. Holding both of my ankles with his huge hands, Mr. Mystery went berserk in the pussy.

"Oh shit, this pussy is good, ma! Awwww shit! I'm about to cum!" he yelled.

"Hold on, baby, I'm almost there. Hit that shit! Hit it hard!" I cried.

He did as I demanded and the buildup was near. Pumping long and hard a couple more times, we both came together just as the heat started drying my truck. Fixing our clothes and adjusting the seats, everything was back to normal when the door opened, indicating the wash was over.

Mr. Mystery Man pulled out of the wash and parked. I got out of the truck to go to the driver's side. He tried to speak, but I got in and pulled off. There was no need for conversation, we'd both gotten what we needed.

I was so exhausted when I got home, I went straight to the bathroom and ran a hot bath. I put my favorite bath salts in so that I could soak and relax. I had put my body through so many sexual activities in the last couple of days, and I was spent.

Slowly undressing and testing the water, I eased down and moaned with my eyes closed.

Thinking about all I'd been through, my body started tingling as soon as I touched my breast. I couldn't believe that I was still horny! I pinched my right nipple and sucked the left at the same time. My clit jumped out of my lower lips like she was playing peek-a-boo. I slid my hand down to my mound, and rotated my fingers on my clit slowly. I picked up the speed, lifting my hips to meet my hand.

"Ooooooohhh, yeah! Shhhhhit!" I cried loud and came harder. My breathing was labored and I had to control it. I washed and rinsed, stepped out of the bathtub and headed straight to bed.

Lying in bed, I smiled to myself. I'd done some amazing shit with my body, and I didn't regret it. I would do it all over again if time permitted. But it wouldn't be any time soon because my life was about to go back to normal, a bitch's leisure days were over. I had to take my ass back to work in the morning, and the only thing on my mind was fuckin'. Let's rub out one more for the road.

The End

The Bitch Next Door
By Misty Holt

"I can't believe we are doing this," Malia muttered as she slid her pink thongs down her pecan colored legs. Her eyes sparkled as she stared at the already naked body of her neighbor.

"I've been waiting for this moment since you moved in." Montrell was openly staring at the toned body of his longtime crush.

"But what about…" Before she could finish her sentence, he had closed the gap between them and taken her erect nipple in his warm mouth. "Ooooh."

He suckled at her breast like a nursing baby. He had been dreaming of the day he could devour the woman next door. He was going to enjoy every moment of playing out his fantasies.

"I want you to forget everything and everyone. All you are to focus on is my voice. My hands. My dick. And my tongue. Tonight, is all about us."

He had removed his mouth from her nipples and replaced it with his cold and bare hands. He had pinched and then kissed her nipples with every word he uttered.

"Mmhmm," she agreed lustfully as she placed her hands over his. It had been months since she enjoyed pleasurable pain and her clit was thumping in anticipation.

Trell raked his eyes over her naked body and felt his dick jump in response. “Lay down,” he demanded in a husky voice.

“K,” she responded as she began backpedaling towards the bed. “But I want you to do something for me.” Not caring what her demand was, he simply nodded his head. “I want you to tell me what you’re doing. I want to hear your voice telling me the pleasure you’re about to cause my body.” She wasn’t sure how he would respond, so to entice him she began lightly rubbing on her moist clit.

“Oh, you’s a nasty bitch, huh?” He placed one hand over hers and began circling her clit, too. The added pressure was causing her juices to flow. He watched in lust as it began making trails down her inner thighs.

“Tonight, I’m whatever and whoever you want me to be,” she gasped as she backed away from his hands. She took the final step backwards, feeling her knees touch the mattress. She never broke eye contact as she lay across the bed.

“Well, let’s get this shit started,” he said as he grabbed his dick, giving it a slight jack. He stared at her hairless pussycat in awe until a twinkle caught his eye. “What’s th…” He couldn’t finish his sentence as he watched her seductively slide a finger into her mouth.

She slid her finger in between her pink lips until it was glistening. “First, I want you to kiss me right…” she placed her wet finger back on her pussy, spreading her folds, “here.”

Montrell was rendered speechless as the culprit for the sparkle was revealed. Malia had a small diamond pierced into her clit. He wasn’t sure how he had missed it, but he couldn’t wait to see if the hearsay was right. He immediately made plans to eat her pussycat with and without the jewel. He had to know if it really increased a woman’s orgasm. Finally finding his own words, he gave her an answer.

“Whatever you want. Tonight is all about pleasure.”

She sat up and grabbed his hand, pulling him closer to the edge of the bed. He obediently dropped to his knees in front of her and stared at her hairless pussy.

“Get this pussy,” she demanded as she grabbed the back of his head. She pulled him to her until she felt his hot breath grace her middle.

“Damn, you even smell good,” he muttered as he lowered his head the rest of the way. He gently flicked his tongue out, letting it tease the tip of her clit.

"Mmmm," she moaned as she lifted her hips to meet his mouth. She pinched and pulled at her nipples as he clamped his lips around her throbbing clit.

"I'm going to stick my tongue in your pussy. I want you to fuck my tongue," his words were almost indecipherable, but she figured it out quickly as she felt him lick from her clit to her asshole before plunging deep into her pussy.

"Oh shit, oh shit," she panted as she began rocking on his tongue. He slid his hands under her thighs as she bucked against his mouth. "I want you to eat this pussy until I cum all over your face. I want to lick it off."

Her words turned him on even more as he brought his mouth back to her clit. The shiver in her body told him that position wouldn't last long. Her pussy came down on his lips as he pursed them. She began to move her body up and down against them slowly. A moan escaped her mouth as she sighed his name. His hands were holding her hips as he finally parted his lips again. She grabbed the back of his head and shoved her pussy in. He let her fuck his face before he began sexily licking from her soaking wet pussy hole to her hard, big clit. He alternated between sucking her clit and tonguing her pussy, sending her body into a frenzy.

Opening his eyes, he noticed she had her head thrown back. Her mouth was open and her nipples were hard as rocks. Her breasts were moving up and down in frantic movements. Pussy juice was sliding down his chin and he remembered her demand. Anxious to feel her lick her own juices from his lips, he decided to up the temperature. He began to suck at her clit as he slid a finger into her pussy and a finger into her ass.

"Ssssss," she sighed as her body immediately reacted. She bucked against him wildly until the room began to dim. She felt the tingle in her clit as the pleasure washed over her body. She pinched and pulled at her nipples until she felt the pressure become too much. Her legs clamped around his neck as her hands grabbed the back of his neck. She rode the wave of pleasure until she could feel him gasping for air.

As she released him from her grip, she gazed at him through lowered lids. Seeing her own juices dripping from his chin had her ready for the next position. She rose up on shaky limbs and crawled to the edge of the bed. She cupped his face as she seductively licked his lips.

"Damn, I taste good," she stated, causing his dick to jump. She grabbed his manhood, jacking it slightly as she kissed and licked her feminine juices from his face. Once she was satisfied with how clean she was she grabbed his hands and forced him into a standing position. "Now, let me return the favor."

The forbidden couple were so into each other, they never noticed the door crack open. They also never saw the two eyes open wide in shock. Samara couldn't believe that her husband of two years was fucking the girl next door. She had been planning on trying to fuck the beautiful girl, too, but had never expressed the urge to her husband. He actually didn't even know she was into females.

Samara's hand dipped into her panties as she watched the woman lick tentatively at the head of Montrell's dick. While she had expected to feel upset, heartbroken even, she was only feeling lust. She pushed the door open a little more so she could have a better view. She removed her skirt and panties and slid to the floor just as she softly sucked the head of his dick. She was completely turned on.

She smiled then bent forward and took the head of his cock into her mouth. It was the most erotic, beautiful thing Sam had ever seen. She took his cock from her mouth, wet her lips then took half of it back into her mouth. She began to slowly suck his dick as she stroked it with her hand. After a few seconds, she paused, and took Samara by surprise. She looked her right in the eye and smiled. Instead of becoming angry, or even worse, embarrassed, she simply nodded. She didn't care that she had been spotted. She just wanted to get her nut, too.

Malia never alerted Montrell to his wife's voyeurism, opting instead to give her the show she wanted.

Samara's eyes couldn't get enough of watching her husband get his dick sucked. A moment later, Malia took his cock from her mouth looked up at him and asked, "Do you like it Trell?" He couldn't even speak choosing instead to simply nod. "Am I a good dick sucker?" Again he nodded. "I need to hear you say it. Let us hear you." She finished her sentence by shoving his dick into her mouth, letting it tease the back of her throat. She was so good at dick sucking, her use of the word *we* never registered in his mind.

"Damn, bitch. Yes. You're a damn good dick sucker. Mmmm, deeper," he moaned as he reached out and palmed the back of her head.

Samara's eyes lowered into slits as she continued to play with her pussy. She wanted to join in but she was enjoying her personal freak show.

She watched as her husband ran his fingers through their neighbor's long tresses. He had begun roughly fucking the girl's face and she was gagging softly. Samara had finally seen enough and decided to open the door. Because Montrell's eyes were closed tightly, he never saw her shadow grace the wall in front of him.

"What the fuck," he damn near screamed as he felt a second mouth close around his nut sack. His eyes shot open and he lowered his head, making instant eye contact with his wife. Knowing he had been busted caused his dick to promptly go flaccid.

"Samara, baby."

He fully expected her to go off, even though she had semi joined in, but instead she just stared up at him. Neither woman had paused her movements, and his dick was overriding his mind. While his mind was yelling, *Stop. It's a setup,* his dick was already back in the game.

"Just enjoy the ride." His wife's words seemed to put him at ease as he slid his hands back into Malia's hair. He tightened his grip as he felt both mouths pleasuring him at once. His head fell back in pleasure as he slow grinded into Malia's mouth.

Samara was enjoying satisfying her husband, but she had a stronger urge to explore the other woman's body. "Let's get in the bed. I have to taste that beautiful pussy."

Montrell was equally taken aback and aroused at the words his woman uttered. Not wanting to ruin the moment, he slowly pulled his dick from Malia's warm mouth. He helped her to her feet and into his marital bed with one swift moment. Once she was settled, he reached down and grabbed his wife by the hands. He pulled her up and kissed her succulent lips. He laughed lightly as he stared at her standing there comfortably in only her shirt and heels.

"Let me help you baby," he said as he slid her shirt over her head. He reached behind her and unclasped her bra, before dropping his mouth to her nipples.

As she arched her back, shoving her titties deeper into his mouth, she felt a soft kiss on the back of her neck. "Grrr," she groaned. She had never been involved in a three-some and she was greatly enjoying the pleasure of having two mouths on her at once.

"Mmmhmmm. I'm ready to join this party, too." Montrell picked his wife up and placed her on the bed beside who was now their guest. Once they were all situated in the bed, Montrell had a moment of regret. He wasn't sure what his consequences were going to be and he no longer felt the carnal pleasure would be worth losing his wife. Before he could express his doubt, his wife had shoved Malia down on her back. He watched with lust and amazement in his eyes as his wife snaked her body up the neighbors. She didn't stop her slow crawl until her neatly trimmed pussy was hovering over the other girl's mouth. She lowered herself slowly until her pussy was smothering Malia.

"I'm about to punish you for fucking my husband." Her words were serious but her tone was playful and sexy. She had no doubt that Malia would be more than willing to pay the cost she had in mind, orgasm after orgasm.

Montrell could tell by the slight jump her body gave that Malia had immediately started licking her pussy. His eyes immediately reverted to tunnel vision and all he could see was Malia's face buried into his wife's pussy. He could, however, hear her slurping and he could also hear how wet Samara was. She began moaning loudly as she bucked against Malia's face. Trell could tell that she was enjoying it by the way her hips were swaying. He wanted to climb in the foray but he didn't want to interrupt what they had going on.

Just as the thought crossed his mind, he felt Samara reach out and grab his steel hard dick. She was holding it, but she was so lost in what Malia was doing to her, all she could do was squeeze. He watched as Malia snaked her hand up and inserted a finger into his wife's ass, an area that for him was uncharted. Any regret he had been feeling quickly flew out of the window right at that moment.

Attempting to make sure he didn't feel excluded, Malia also reached out to grab his pleasure stick. When Samara felt her soft hands reaching for the engorged penis she was holding, but doing nothing with, she quickly withdrew her own small hand. Malia was stroking his dick slowly but firmly. But she never faltered from making love to his wife with her mouth and fingers.

Samara suddenly moaned loudly and attempted to rise from Malia's face. Malia quickly released her hold on Trell's dick and wrapped her strong arms around the other woman's waist. She held her in place as she sucked on her clit with a tighter suction. Trell decided to just sit back and watch the action. He knew his wife was a squirter and he knew the orgasm that was building was intense. She rocked her pussy harder and faster against the other woman's mouth as the air was sucked from her body. She tightened all over and he knew what was next.

Just as he expected, her spine stiffened before she released the breath she seemed to have been holding. "Aaaah," she yelled as her fluids came gushing out. It felt like someone had opened a faucet right above Malia's head, but she never slowed her sucking. She wanted to suck the soul out of the woman's body. Once her shaking had slowed down, Malia released her grips on the woman's hips and let her fall from her face. Malia and Trell stared at her as her intense orgasm subsided.

When she regained her composure, she seemed to remember that her husband was in the room as well. She hungrily eyed his hard dick before slithering over to where he sat with his legs spread.

She quickly took him in her mouth and began to give him head like she had never done before. Not wanting to miss anything, Malia rushed over and began sucking his balls as his wife did earlier. He felt her tongue licking his balls and felt her gently sucking them into her mouth. He was watching both women pleasing him, and he felt his toes curl up. He knew his wife didn't like to swallow and he knew his nut was coming fast, so he nudged her head away.

Then she did something he wasn't expecting, even under the circumstances. Still holding his member in her hand, she grabbed the back of Malia's neck and shoved it in her mouth. Malia didn't even flinch, she just finished giving him the pleasure his wife had started. She used one hand to lightly jack his dick and the other to softly massage his balls.

Samara stretched out and he could see that she was watching intently. She looked into his eyes and smiled really big.

Samara needed more attention so she climbed behind Malia and mounted her plum ass. She began grinding her still wet pussy on the girl as she was pleasing her husband. The visual on top of the fire ass top he was receiving, was pushing him over the edge. He finally couldn't stand it anymore. He looked down at Malia, who was staring straight into his eyes, and told her he was ready. “Oh shit. I’m about cum.” They never stopped what they were doing as his face balled up tighter than his toes.

His wife looked at him with a grin on her face. “Give it to her, daddy. She wants it,” she spoke for the other girl as she was still grinding against her ass.

Malia began sucking harder and pumping her hand faster. He couldn’t hold back any longer as he shot his hot load of cum in to her mouth. She didn’t cease sucking as she swallowed all of his sweet juices down her throat. When it got to be too much, she picked her head up and watched the rest of his cum ooze from the head.

As he finished, his wife rose from her back, allowing her to raise from his body with a smirk on her face. Samara ended up next to the two and grabbed Malia’s face, pulling her in for a deep kiss. The two of them were sharing his cum and Samara's juices in their mouths, and he was enthralled.

They continued to kiss until Samara laid back on the bed. She was lying on her back and the other woman moved on top of her. They were kissing passionately and their hands were roaming up and down each other’s bodies. He perked up as their guest took his wife’s hand and guided it between her legs. Trell watched as she slid her finger inside

Malia's pussy. His dick jumped as he heard them both moan.

He changed his position so he could see better. Just as he got comfortable, she inserted a second finger and started moving her hand faster. Malia reached down and grabbed her hand and moved it up to her own mouth. She licked her juices from his wife's fingers and pushed her hand down again. She did that a couple more times before changing it up. The next time, she pushed them towards Samara's mouth. Once again, he really expected her to balk and say no. But she didn't. She pushed her wet fingers into her mouth and sucked the pussy juices from them.

The finger tasting went on for several minutes. Soon she was doing it all on her own. She would push her fingers inside the girl's wet pussy. She would get them wet and then raise them to Malia's mouth. Then she would do it all again and raise them to her own mouth. He was hard again before he knew it.

Finally, she raised her wet fingers to his mouth and pushed them in. He quickly sucked the juices from her fingers. She smiled at him drunkenly.

Trell decided to be brave. "Baby, I really want to watch you go down on her." He expected her to go off and end the night's festivities, but she continued to surprise him.

"Oh, yeah? You'd like that?"

With surprise in his eyes, he nodded his head. "Yes, babe. Very much so."

She replied with her own head nod. "Well, I wouldn't want to disappoint you. Tonight's all about dreams and fantasies, right?" She moved in between her legs as if she had done it a million times before. He watched as she lowered her head and began to slowly and gently lick and suck at Malia's pussy. Samara's legs were spread wide, so he moved searching for a better view of his wife's tongue game.

Surprisingly, it didn't take long for Malia to start moaning and pushing against his wife's mouth. She suddenly arched her back and bucked her hips as her impending orgasm built. Thinking of what caused her own pleasure, Samara continued to suck hard on the candy coated clit. It seemed only seconds passed before Malia was shooting her hot juices into her mouth. Samara didn't stop, though. She was still gently licking the neighbor's pussy and sucking her lips into her mouth.

Malia moaned, "If you're going to keep doing that, then you should turn around and let me do you at the same time."

For the first time Samara looked unsure. *What the hell? I've gone this far.* As she thought of all the things they had done already, she quickly shifted her body around so that she was straddling

Malia's face. She hurried to lower her pussy on her waiting mouth.

Trell felt like he had died and gone to heaven. A night of cheating had quickly turned into a fantasy come true. He turned his body around so he was behind his wife. He took his dick in his hand and guided it into his wife. She gasped when she felt him enter her. He wondered if she could tell that he was harder than he'd ever been.

Malia continued to suck his wife's clit, and he could look down and see her face and tongue every time he moved. To him, it was an amazing sight.

Occasionally, he would feel Malia's tongue on his balls and that just heightened the pleasure!

Samara began to moan louder, causing the other woman to reach her hands behind him. She grabbed his ass and started forcefully slamming him into the pussy.

"I want you to make her cum all over my face," she demanded as she lifted the woman's hips from her face. She was shouting encouragement in between tongue flickers. "Fuck her! Make her cum! Fuck her harder!"

He felt Samara's pussy muscles contract and knew she was cumming hard. She arched her back and let out a loud moan. "Mmmmm. Oooooh." It seemed to go on forever. He tried to ride the wave of pleasure with her, but the contractions of her orgasm forced him out.

As soon as he was out of the pussy, he felt Malia take him into her mouth. She carefully sucked all of his wife's juices from his member as his wife attempted to crawl forward on shaky legs.

Watching her struggle, he pulled his dick out of Malia's mouth giving her room to maneuver. She rolled off the top of the pile and laid flat on her back. She was panting as she attempted to catch her breath.

Malia stared at the rise and fall in open admiration. She slowly crawled over to her and began to softly suck her lips. "I wanna taste my pussy on your tongue." Having no energy to protest, Samara just parted her lips. Their kiss had Trell rocked up again. He wanted back in the mix, but he was content watching the two women. As they began to paw at each other, he began to slowly stroke his meat.

Tired of the kissing, Malia moved on top of Samara in a 69 position. She smiled at them both. "Now it's my turn. I wanna feel this golden tongue and that big ole dick." She lowered her pussy onto the waiting mouth below her before making eye contact with Trell. "I want you to fuck me hard. Hurt me." She lowered her head and began devouring the pussy beneath her.

Trell didn't hesitate to climb behind her. He threw his head back as his wife grabbed his dick and guided it into the tight pussy in front of him.

"Awwww," he groaned. He remembered her telling him that she hadn't had sex in a while but he was nowhere near ready for the tight wetness he had slid in to. He had to stop for a moment to regain his composure. He knew if he moved it would be over before he made two good strokes. There was no way he could let his wife offer more pleasure than him. Once he got it together and starting stroking, he could see his wife was watching every inch slide in and out. He started fucking her just the way she asked. As he reached his hands out and wrapped them around her neck, he saw that his wife was going as hard as he was.

He knew there was no way he would last long, so he stroked long and hard. He needed to make Malia cum before he did. Just as he thought he had won the battle, his wife reached up and began massaging his balls. "Ahhhh, hell," he mumbled as he felt the tingle start at his toes.

He had just given up hope of Malia beating him to ecstasy when she arched her back and groaned. There was no reason to wonder what was happening because she began screaming. "Yes. Oh, God, yes. Right there. Bitch, eat this pussy. Ooooh, Trell, fuck me, daddy." Her pussy clamped down even harder as her orgasm took control of her body.

He knew his nut was rising, so he made two more strokes before pulling out. Right as he did, he exploded all over Malia's ass. It was so explosive it dripped from her ass, down her pussy, and on to his wife's face.

He moved his hand onto his dick and pumped it hard. More cum shot all over the women, managing to turn him on all over again.

His wife managed to surprise him once again as she lifted her head and began licking his sperm from the other woman's pussy, causing them both to moan out. Once she had her cleaned to her liking, she pushed her off her body, causing her to bump Trell. He had already been struggling to support himself, so he just toppled over. Malia let her body fall in between the husband and wife.

They all laid their gasping for air as their chests rose and fell rapidly. "Damn." Malia was the first to be able to speak. "I wish we could stay and do this again."

"You should. We should." Samara also hadn't had enough and had been planning her persuasion speech.

"Yea." Trell kept his answer short. He didn't have another round in him, but he could definitely watch.

"I have to get home before…"

Bam. Bam. Bam.

Her reply was interrupted by a heavy banging.

"My husband gets home."

The End

Total Domination
By Chazae

Chapter 1

He pulled his all black Corvette around the circular driveway of the address that Karen had given him. He was told that the party would start at 6pm. It was now 7:30. He was sure that the party would be in full swing by now. When he stepped out of the car, the cold winter breeze bit down into his bones. He put on his black overcoat and scarf to keep warm. He handed the valet his keys and a crisp one-hundred-dollar bill. He made his way to the door and found it very odd that there was no loud music being played.

"This is supposed to be a party. Where is the music?" he thought to himself as he walked to the door. He turned around and saw all of the exotic cars that were lined up in the parking area. He just figured that the walls were soundproof as to not disturb the closest neighbors. The house itself was made of brown bricks and had huge windows. The curtains were closed. He couldn't tell if people were inside or not because the curtains were a thick silk grey. He raised his hand and used the door knocker to announce his arrival.

A woman in a short grey dress came to the

door. She wore a mask over her face. It was the kind of mask that one would wear at a masquerade ball. She was very curvy and her skin was the color of peanut butter with a hint of chocolate.

"Welcome, sir. May I please see your invitation?" she asked him casually. He reached into his pocket and found the gold envelope with the black seal. Karen had told him specifically not to open it.

The woman took the envelope and broke the seal. She pulled out the card and read it to herself. She looked at him and smiled.

"Thank you so much, Mister Broadmoor. Please, follow me."

She led him to a coat room at the end of a short hallway.

"Remove your coat and shirt." He wanted to protest removing his shirt, but her demanding tone made him think better of it and do as he was told.

Once he was done, his dark skin was bare. His abs were cut into the perfect six pack and his arms were slightly chiseled. The woman looked at him and licked her lips. She reached up and placed a black collar with a long leash around his neck.

"What are you doing?" he yelled.

"Silence! You are hers now. I am your handler. You will refer to me as ma'am. You will do as you are told while under this roof. Any disobedience will result in punishment. Do I make myself clear?"

"Yes," he said.

Whack! Out of nowhere, she had a whip in her hand, the kind that a horse jockey uses to make a horse run.

"What did you say, my pet?" she said with a smile.

"Yes, ma'am."

"Good. Now come, we mustn't keep your Mistress waiting. Do not speak until she speaks to you."

She led him quietly through the house, where other men were collared and women led them by the leash. They walked down a set of stairs to what appeared to be a throne room. Naked men knelt with their heads down while women stood nearby. He looked at the woman who sat on the throne and couldn't believe his eyes.

"Why is that one still fully clothed?" she asked while pointing at him. "Strip."

Paul Broadmoor did as he was told without hesitation. He had made a couple of errors and had been punished for it on the way down. The woman stood up and walked over to where he stood. She wore red leather clothes and red leather boots. The sound of them click clacked on the floor. She had a long whip in her hand.

"Say my name, Paul," she said as she took the leash from his handler.

"Karen," he said softly.

"Wrong answer. I am going to have so much fun breaking you," she said as she raised her whip. "Remember my last name. That's the safe word."

"Karen, what is going on?" Paul asked as he stood with his mouth open at her. *Whack!* His question was met with at sharp swat from her whip.

"Silence!" she said in a demanding tone. "Melissa, why is this one so disrespectful?"

"I do not know, Mistress. I have informed him of these things and yet he still refuses to listen," Melissa responded.

"Fine. Take him to the dungeon and prepare him for his breaking."

"Yes, Mistress," Melissa said and took the leash from Karen's hand.

Chapter 2

Melissa led him down another long hallway that they had not been down yet. The sounds of men in the throes of passion and women with cracking whips filled the hollow walkway.

"You have embarrassed me, my pet," Melissa said as she tugged on the leash sharply. "You made me look like I did not have a grip on you. Now you will be punished severely. And the only way to get out of this is to speak the safe word. Do you remember it?"

"Yes, ma'am. I didn't know that I would embarrass you."

"You did. But that is fine. I will break you. I am going to break you so well that when you are with the Mistress, you will beg for me. When you leave this house, you will want no other woman except for me. Understood?"

"Yes," he said. Melissa pulled the leash hard until his face was right in front of hers.

"You will learn respect. You will beg for my mercy. You will scream. You will do as you are told. This collar around your neck means that you are mine. You are my pet."

"But what is the safe word, ma'am?"

"Oh, how easy one forgets," she laughed.

She led him to a closed door, took out a single golden key, and unlocked it. Once inside, she turned on the light switch and the red light poured down from the bulb above.

Inside of the room, there were all kinds of devices. Whips hung on the walls. There were a couple of leather floggers that hung limply on a rack. There were black masks on mannequin heads that zipped up on the back and only had holes for the eyes, mouth, and nose. There were a couple of chairs that sat in the middle of the room. A pair of chains hung loosely from the ceiling and another pair lay beneath them on the floor. In one corner of the room there was a bed with handcuffs that were attached to the four bedposts.

"Now, my pet. I am going to tell you what to do. When I tell you to do it, you will do it with urgency. Failure to do so will result in harsh punishment. When you do as you are told, you will be rewarded. Do I make myself clear?" Melissa said to him.

He did not speak.

Whack! She struck him with the leather jockey's whip. "When I ask a question you are to answer it."

"Yes, ma'am."

"Good boy. Now go put a mask on. I can't stand your face."

Paul was not an unattractive man. He was quite the opposite. Women flocked to him. He resembled the rapper T.I. with LL Cool J's lips and tongue. He was always caught licking his lips at some woman. That was always a few hours before he would have them moaning his name while digging her pussy out with his nine-inch dick in his bed. Paul was what some considered a lady's man.

Despite all of that, Paul shuffled as quickly as he could to the mannequins where the masks were. He chose one and put it over his face. When he looked through the eyes, he saw Melissa coming towards him.

Whack! Paul winced in pain as the whip crossed his bare chest. He was confused.

"Did I tell my pet to put that one on?" she asked with a sadistic grin.

"No, ma'am. You just said to put on a mask," Paul said as he looked at her.

"Exactly, and do not look at me. I told you that I don't like your face. Put on the red one in the middle," she said as she pointed at a specific one. Paul rushed over to it, removed the one he had on, and put the one she told him to put on with the quickness. He rushed back to her with his head down.

"Kneel, my pet," she said with her hands on her leather clad hips. He did as he was told. "Good. Does my pet want to please me?"

"Yes, ma'am," he said in a muffled tone as she walked over and zipped the mask up in the back.

"Oh you will please me. Do you want me to

please you, my pet?" Paul thought about this question.

Melissa Carrington worked in the same office as he did. She was a very quiet woman. He had tried on numerous occasions to get her to bed with him. Her plump titties sat high on their own. Paul knew that she never wore a bra. He had seen her big brown nipples through some of her blouses so many times. She loved wearing leggings and summer dresses with no undergarments on. Sometimes, he would sneak a picture of her and go to the bathroom and jack off to it. Needless to say, he wanted her bad. But the pain that he was experiencing right now, was not what he envisioned as the time of his life with her bouncing up and down and screaming his name while her creamy pussy gushed its juices all over him.

"Yes, ma'am," he replied calmly.

"Good. But until you pay for making me look like a fool in front of the Mistress, you will only find pleasure in pleasing me. Do you understand?"

"Yes, ma'am."

She walked to one of the chairs and sat in it. She crossed her thick thighs and raised a finger to him, beckoning for him to approach her. He stood up and walked to her. *Whack!*

"Did I tell you to stand? Or did I tell you to approach me?"

"Ma'am, you beckoned for me to come to you."

"You walk your happy ass back over there and you get back on your knees and come to me as you are supposed to. My pets do not walk. They crawl."

He walked back to the spot where he was kneeling and knelt again. He glanced up at her and she beckoned him to her again. He crawled with his head down until he was directly in front of her.

"Now I want you to remove my shoes with your hand. Then I want you to rub my feet."

This made him cringe. Word around the water cooler at Tyson and Associates was that Paul, being the sweetest gentlest lover that any woman could dream of, had a problem with feet. Most of the women who had slept with him would go all out of their way to get their feet looking perfect just to test the theory that he would never touch them. No matter how many times they tried, he would never even so much as look at their pretty pedicured toes.

"Ma'am, I don't want to touch your feet."

"Oh, I know, my pet. I know that you don't want to. Let me give you this bit of information. For things that you are uncomfortable with doing, then the safe word is jungle. Can you remember that word, Paul? Jungle."

"Jungle. Yes, ma'am."

"Good, now I said to remove my shoes and rub my feet."

"Rub your feet, ma'am? Jungle," he said respectfully.

"Very well. Remove my shoes."

Paul was shocked that she respected his wishes so easily. He thought that he would be met with another lash from the whip. He was not.

He obliged her by removing her shoes. When he looked at her pretty feet, he smiled. *It can't be that bad,* he thought to himself. He raised one of his hands and he gently touched her feet. He started rubbing them in a round motion. Melissa sighed softly as she smiled. Paul was in shock at how soft her feet were. They did not stink nor were they all crusty like he thought all feet were. She moaned a little louder.

"Enough, my pet," she said to him as she was nearing the beginning stages of ecstasy. He removed his hands from her feet and looked down at the floor. "How did my feet feel in your hands?"

"They felt soft and welcoming, ma'am," he replied proudly.

"Perfect. You see, Paul, it is not so bad to please others before you get pleased," she said to him. "Now, I want you to play with my kitty. Do not worry, she is shaved and cleaned. Do not stop until I say to stop." She stood up and removed her pants, exposing her pretty caramel mound.

He reached his hand up and placed it to the slit of her pussy. The light moisture of it made the tip of his finger wet. He started with one finger to get a feel for the inside of her. She threw her head back and gasped when his finger entered.

He stroked the inside of her pussy walls with his manicured finger slowly. After she was soaking wet, he inserted another finger inside. As he slid his fingers inside of her, he took his thumb and circled it around her clit. Melissa could not contain herself. She moaned loudly.

"Yes, Paul. That's my spot," she moaned. "Don't stop." He was glad to obey her order. He stroked her pussy faster. "Fuck, Paul!" she cried out. "Make mama cum!"

Paul slid another finger inside of her pussy and played with it, touching her G-spot.

"Fuck!" she yelled as she threw her head back. Her juices flowed from her pussy all down his arm as he continued to stroke her pussy. "Enough!" she yelled. Paul stopped and removed his fingers from her. "Lick it, Paul."

He looked up at her wet pussy and licked his lips. He placed his lips around her exposed clit and began to lick it. He rolled his tongue around it as he sucked on her pussy lips like a lollipop. She placed her hands on his head. She could not deny that his head game was on point.

There were plenty of days that she had sat at her desk and envisioned this very moment. She was all of a sudden mad at herself for not getting to him before the other bitches in the office. She could never have made him do the things that she wanted him to do under any other circumstances. She was a true dominatrix and she was not used to letting any man have his way with her without her express permission.

Melissa kept her hand on his head and pushed his face deeper into her pussy, and forcing him to lick it harder, which he did with no hesitation.

"God damn, baby! Lick it for mama!" she said just as she was cumming down his throat. He slurped her juices faithfully. "Stop. Stand up," she said breathlessly.

Paul got up from his knees and looked down at his erect manhood. Melissa grabbed the leash and led him to the chains that hung from the ceiling. On the end of them there were black leather cuffs with fur on the inside.

"Raise your hands above your head, Paul," Melissa commanded. "I promise the pain will be pleasurable."

"Yes, ma'am," he said as he raised his hands above his head.

Melissa walked over to him and placed his hands inside of the cuffs and closed them. She placed his ankles in the cuffs that were on the chains on the floor. She walked over to a switch on the wall and flipped it. The chains on the ceiling started to raise, elevating him a couple of feet off of the floor.

"Ma'am?" he questioned. "What is going on?"

"Shhh, just relax. I promise that you will find pleasure in this."

"Yes, ma'am," he said, wanting to say the safe word but he thought better of it.

Melissa walked over and grabbed one of the floggers off of the rack. She smiled at him as she walked back to him with the tassels of the flogger swinging wildly. When she got to him, she walked behind him and ran the tassels softly down his back. He gasped softly at the feeling of the soft leather sliding down his back.

"Now, Paul. I am going to hit you softly with this. It will be uncomfortable at first. But I am not going to hurt you."

"Wait, Melissa," a voice said from the door. Melissa stopped and looked towards the door.

"Hello, Mistress," she said to Karen as she walked in with another woman.

"Hello, Paul," Karen said to him. "Say hello to Geraldine."

"Hello, Geraldine," he said.

Geraldine was a tall, light skinned woman. She had her hair in a natural style. She was very thick and curvy. She had a collar around her neck and Karen had a leash on her as well. Her dark brown eyes were stuck on Karen.

"Geraldine, Paul said hello. Do not be rude.

Speak back to the gentleman," Karen commanded.

"My apologies, Mistress," she said diverting her eyes to Paul. "Good evening, Paul."

"Melissa, unchain him. I have been watching and I think he can be rewarded properly."

"As you wish, Mistress." Melissa walked over to the switch and flipped it down and lowered Paul back to the floor. She then walked back to Paul and removed the cuffs from around his wrists and ankles.

"Paul, what is my name?" Karen said to him.

"Mistress," he replied obediently.

"Do you remember the safe word?"

"Yes, Mistress."

"Good. Now go lay on the bed on your back." Paul walked to the bed and lay down on his back. "Geraldine, handcuff his hands and feet."

"Yes, Mistress," Geraldine said as she rushed over and did as she was instructed.

"Now we will seduce this man until he screams all of our names."

Melissa smiled as she walked over and grabbed his dick in her hand and began stroking it slowly.

"You will not cum until I say you can. Do you understand?" Karen said to him.

"Yes, Mistress."

"Geraldine, suck his nipples."

Geraldine walked over and placed her mouth on his small brown nipples and began to suck them. Karen took the flogger and rubbed it on his chest to his stomach as Melissa stroked his dick. Melissa stopped stroking it and took it into her mouth and began to suck his dick. Karen took the handle of the flogger and rubbed Melissa's pussy with it.

"Do you like that, Melissa?"

"Yessssss, Mistress," she hissed with a mouthful of Paul's dick in her throat.

"Geraldine, sit on his face. Paul suck her pussy." Geraldine stopped sucking his nipples and sat on his face towards Karen. Paul wanted to reach up and part her pussy lips with his hands, but was met with resistance from the handcuffs.

The three of them, Melissa, Geraldine and Paul, engaged in the threesome as Karen watched while she played with her own pussy. She was not greedy but she had wanted to fuck Paul since the first time she lay eyes on him.

"Melissa, let me ride that dick," Karen demanded. "Remember, Paul. Do not cum until I say so."

Melissa stopped sucking his dick and Karen straddled his dick and slowly slid down on it. At first the feeling of him between her pussy lips made her pussy get extra wet. She began to slowly grind on his dick, up and down. Paul couldn't move because he still had Geraldine's pussy on his face. She had come twice just from his tongue alone. Melissa walked over to her and started sucking on her titty. She couldn't help it. Geraldine came again from the sheer feeling of Melissa's tongue on her nipple and Paul's tongue in her pussy.

Karen sped up and was taking the longest ride, up and down, in and out of her pussy. She took pleasure and had a creamy orgasm on his dick.

"Ooooh shit," she screamed out as she had her orgasm. "Cum for your Mistress, Paul." She got off of his dick and started to stroke him quickly. His dick throbbed in her hand as she felt him about to erupt. She opened her mouth and took his entire load in her mouth and swallowed every drop of it. "Mmmmmm, yess, Paul. Give your Mistress all of that milky nut."

After ten minutes, Paul was uncuffed and was given his clothes back.

"You are more than welcome into my home any time you desire to be fucked, Paul," Melissa said. "But you must remember that what happens here, never leaves here."

"Yes, ma'am. Not a single soul shall know of this experience."

"Good. Now have a good evening," she said as she led him down the corridor to the front door. She handed him his coat and opened the door for him. He walked out into the morning air.

He did not know how long he had been there

nor did he care. He had a very intense experience. He would go into the office and look at the three women in a different manner.

He knew their secret was one that even if he did desire to tell anyone else, no one would believe it.

***

A few weeks later, Paul was invited back to what he dubbed as the Grey Zone. After taking off his jacket and shirt and receiving his collar, he was led to the head mistress. But something in him this time caused him to rebel. When told to do something, he said no and was punished accordingly. Karen was intrigued. She wanted to know what had gotten into him. When she went to strike him the third time, he caught her wrist in midair and twisted it so that her ass was nestled in his groin area. She could feel his snake creeping down his leg.

"Now, Karen, we did this your way the first time. Now it's my show! You will do what I say, when I say, or there will be *consequences*! Do I make myself clear?" he whispered in her ear with so much authority and power that there was a puddle beneath her feet.

Karen had no idea what she'd just gotten herself into, but soon enough, she would be made an example of when the dominator became dominated.

"Now you listen…" before she could utter another word, she was against the wall with a strong hand around her neck, delicate but firm.

"I asked you a fucking question. Do I make myself clear? The only words you should be saying are yes Daddi! Now let me hear it!" Paul shouted while staring in her eyes with such intensity that she orgasmed again.

Drip.

Drip.

"Yeeesssss, Daddi!" she moaned and she wasn't even getting the dick yet.

Without breaking eye contact he asked, "Did I tell you that you can cum?" He still had a hand around her neck when he moved her from the wall to the bed.

Her mind was in a haze at this point and she didn't know if she was coming or going. This was not how it was supposed to happen. She was supposed to be in control so she was upset that her body manipulated itself and succumbed to his demands.

"No Daddi!" she stammered, still feeling the effects of the orgasm, but she knew another was brewing. It was inevitable.

She had never felt anything like she was experiencing. She was used to men bowing at her command. But the feeling that was possessing her at the moment was something new and something euphoric.

Paul looked at the expression on her face, one that read pure ecstasy. He had her right where he wanted her! Without another word, Paul withdrew his hand, got up, and looked at her. They stared at each other in silence for a good two minutes before Paul turned on his heels and proceeded towards the door.

"Hold the hell up!" Karen shouted, "What the hell do you think you're doing? You are not about to just leave me here like this!"

Paul looked over his shoulder and said, "Watch me," and walked out the door.

Chapter 3

A few days later, Paul was asked by Karen to stop by her home that evening after work. He simply answered, “I'll think about it,” and went on about his day. Karen was steaming mad. She still caught goosebumps thinking about the last time he was at her house. And for him to dismiss her the way he did had her mad and sexually aroused. She was also sexually frustrated because no one had been able to get her to that point ever since that night. Karen packed up her things and left the office for the day. She could not stand to look at Paul for two reasons: she was mad at him, and he was turning her on.

Karen climbed into her cocaine white BMW 745 and left smoke in her wake, peeling out of the parking lot. She needed something to calm her nerves so she reached into her glove department and pulled out a pre-rolled backwoods filled with some sour diesel pressure. Once she lit the spliff, she inhaled the smoke deep into her lungs and held it. She felt a difference immediately.

Karen stopped by the liquor store for a bottle of Jose Gold and a pack of backwoods. She predicted that she was going to have a long night. Karen drove the rest of the way to her home. When she entered her property she immediately noticed Paul's all black Corvette in her driveway, looking sexy like him. *"The nerve of this bastard!"* she thought to herself. She parked her baby, grabbed her things, and proceeded to the door, completely ignoring Paul on the way.

Paul was completely perplexed. He thought he let it be known the last time how shit would be from then on, but obviously she missed the memo. So he thought he would remind her.

Karen unlocked the door, walked in, and tried to close the door quickly, but was unsuccessful. Paul had his foot in the door. He looked at her with the same intensity of the night he'd left her hot and bothered.

"You will not walk past me like you didn't see me. So I suggest your little black ass get some act right and get from behind this door!" he said in a low but firm tone.

Karen slowly moved from behind the door and proceeded to her kitchen to fix herself a much needed drink. "Didn't I leave you at the office?" she asked with attitude.

"No, you thought you did. But the lust in your eyes let me know that you would be leaving soon because you knew I would follow you," he replied cockily.

Karen rolled her eyes and proceeded to fix her drink. She moved around the kitchen with such grace and sexiness, Paul felt his mini-me awakening in his slacks. Karen wanted to be petty and entice him so she dropped ice on purpose while getting it out of the freezer for her drink. Once she sat her glass down, she turned around and bent over with her perfect round *Fluffy Cloud*, as she called it, facing Paul, and picked up the ice. She stood up and continued to fix her drink, turning around with a straight face and asking Paul if he would like a drink.

He accepted while continuing to watch her act like he wasn't impacting her pussy at that point, even with his presence. Once she finished fixing their drinks, she placed his in front of him, along with a plate of limes and some salt, and then excused herself to get comfortable while she left him there with a hard dick, tequila, and his thoughts.

Karen went to her bedroom and closed the door. She leaned against it and took a big sip of her Tequila to settle her nerves. At that point, she didn't know what was going on with her body. No man had ever made her feel that way. She prided herself on being in control, but this time she felt she bit off more than she could chew. She went to her dresser and pulled out her bed wear. She didn't want to seem too desperate so she settled on some boy shorts and a tank top.

She then grabbed her drink and a pre-rolled blunt out of her case with a lighter and went to her bathroom to start herself a bath. She didn't care that she had company, she was going to relax for a minute. She didn't want to face Paul yet, anyway, until she had time to gather her thoughts. Once her bath water was done and she added her favorite fragrances, she submerged herself and then lit up her spliff.

Downstairs, Paul was getting irritated after ten minutes passed, so he downed his drink, took a shot, and fixed another drink, then proceeded up the stairs. Once in Karen's bedroom, he removed his shoes, shirt, and pants. He then made himself comfortable with his drink and remote on the bed while Karen tended to her hygiene.

Ten minutes later, Karen removed herself from the tub, grabbed her huge Egyptian cotton towel, and dried herself. She proceeded to her bedroom where she jumped once she realized that Paul had made himself at home, barely blinking at her presence. She went over to her dresser and grabbed her Shea butter body butter and dropped her towel before heading to the bench at the foot of her bed. She was a ball of nerves as she started sexily and seductively applying the cream to her body.

Paul was watching her every move, unbeknownst to her. When she stood up to return her body butter, Paul was already up and in her space. She tried to control herself by backing up and proceeding to put on her clothes. Paul stood there and watched her as she dressed and grabbed another spliff out of her box. She hadn't planned on smoking another one, but Paul had her head all over the place.

After she lit the spliff, she inhaled a good bit of smoke and before she exhaled, Paul placed his soft succulent lips to hers, took the shotgun, and proceeded to tongue her down. She was shocked. She didn't even know he smoked. Without breaking their kiss, Paul took the spliff from her hand, put it out, and then picked her up and carried her to the bed. He gently laid her down and then broke the kiss. He looked into her eyes while removing the clothes she'd put on not too long ago. Her breathing became short and choppy.

Out of nowhere, her domination tried to make itself known. Paul peeped game but quickly shut that shit down by saying, "If you move, I promise you will regret it! Look at me, Karen, tell me if you think I'm bluffing!"

Karen backed down but in that moment she had her first orgasm with the same intensity as the last time he was there and she was in heaven. She was almost tempted to rebel just to receive punishment, but she, the dominating, was once again being dominated. By the time she came down, Paul was standing there stroking his monster while looking at her with much lust and wanting.

"Spread them!" he said in a raspy, sexy voice.

Karen did as she was told, exposing her pretty

pink pearl that he had been dreaming of until it gave him blue balls. He took his tongue and ran it along her thighs, leaving wet kisses along the way, like a road map to paradise. Once he reached her pie, he sucked on her clit like a baby with a pacifier while she squirmed underneath him moaning loud enough for her neighbors to know his name. He then took his finger and began to finger fuck her while sucking on her pearl.

He removed his finger and put it in her mouth while maneuvering his tongue down to her ass and back up to her forbidden treasure. Karen was trying to run because his tongue game was far too much for her. He kissed up her body and sucked on her chocolate drops called nipples while she begged him to fuck her.

"Shut up! You didn't ask for permission to cum. For that you have to pay! Turn over, face down, ass up! Now!"

Karen did as she was told, even though she wanted let the dam loose. But she didn't know what was already in store for her, so she was humble. Paul teased her pussy while running the head of his monster up and down her slit, getting it more gushy than she was already was. He inserted the head then pulled it out. He did it again.

"If you don't put him in…"

She didn't have time to finish her rant because he was deep with his hand around her neck, saying in her ear, "Or you'll what? Huh? This what you want?" he asked while reaching depths in her she didn't know existed. He continued to rock all nine inches in her while all she could do was moan and scream out to the Gods for mercy.

"That's not my name!" he belted. He released her neck and started to pound her box with deep fast strokes. "What's my name?" he roared.

"Oh! My! Daddi!" she screamed.

He smacked her ass so hard it stung but that made her body squirt all over his thighs and stomach. He flipped her over without removing himself and continued to fuck her while looking straight in her eyes. She tried to close hers. "Open your eyes Karen! Let me see what you're trying to hide!" he smoothly said.

She opened her eyes and moaned so sexily that he had to slow down before he came. When she felt the shift in his speed, she tried to flip him over so she could take control. But she was mistaken.

Paul realized she still didn't realize who was running the show, so he continued to fuck her and asked, "Who run this shit?" while grabbing her around the neck.

If she answered, she would be submitting herself to a man sexually for the first time in her life. Her silence caused Paul to lift her legs on his shoulders and go deeper than she could think of. He asked again, "Who run this shit, Karen?" while squeezing a little harder.

She felt her orgasm reaching and realized she didn't want to let this feeling go so she submitted to his total domination and replied, “You do, Daddi! You run this pussy! Can I please cum, Daddi?”

Hearing her submit to his will caused his member to throb and had him ready to bust. He answered, “Yes, mami! Cum with Daddi!”

She let the dam loose and they came together with so much passion he was sure they made a baby! He continued to pump until her pussy sucked him dry. She laid there, weak and out of energy.

She looked at him and asked, “What did you do to me?”

He simply replied, “I dominated a Dominatrix!”

The End

Stay Connected with Us!

Text **LOCKDOWN** to 22828 to stay up-to-date with new releases, sneak peaks, contests and more…

Thank you!

Coming Soon from Lock Down Publications/Ca$h Presents

BOW DOWN TO MY GANGSTA

By **Ca$h & Jamaica**

TORN BETWEEN TWO

By **Coffee**

CUM FOR ME **III**

By **Ca$h & Company**

BLOOD OF A BOSS **IV**

By **Askari**

BRIDE OF A HUSTLA **III**

By **Destiny Skai**

WHEN A GOOD GIRL GOES BAD **II**

By **Adrienne**

LOVE & CHASIN' PAPER **II**

By **Qay Crockett**

THE HEART OF A GANGSTA **II**

By **Jerry Jackson**

TO DIE IN VAIN **II**

By **ASAD**

THE BOSS MAN'S DAUGHTERS **II**

By **Aryanna**

UNBREAK MY HEART

By **Misty Holt**

A DOPEBOY'S PRAYER **II**

By **Eddie "Wolf" Lee**

Available Now

(CLICK TO PURCHASE)

RESTRAING ORDER **I & II**

By **CA$H & Coffee**

LOVE KNOWS NO BOUNDARIES **I II & III**

By **Coffee**

LAY IT DOWN **I & II**

LAST OF A DYING BREED

By **Jamaica**

PUSH IT TO THE LIMIT

By **Bre' Hayes**

BLOOD OF A BOSS **I II & III**

By **Askari**

THE STREETS BLEED MURDER **I, II & III**

THE HEART OF A GANGSTA

By **Jerry Jackson**

CUM FOR ME

CUM FOR ME 2

An **LDP Erotica Collaboration**

BRIDE OF A HUSTLA **I & II**

By **Destiny Skai**

WHEN A GOOD GIRL GOES BAD

By **Adrienne**

A GANGSTER'S REVENGE **I II III & IV**

THE BOSS MAN'S DAUGHTERS

A SAVAGE LOVE **I & II**

By **Aryanna**

A DOPEBOY'S PRAYER

By **Eddie "Wolf" Lee**

WHAT ABOUT US **I & II**

NEVER LOVE AGAIN

THUG ADDICTION

By **Kim Kaye**

THE KING CARTEL **I, II & III**

By **Frank Gresham**

THESE NIGGAS AIN'T LOYAL **I, II & III**

By **Nikki Tee**

GANGSTA SHYT **I II &III**

By **CATO**

THE ULTIMATE BETRAYAL

By **Phoenix**

DON'T FU#K WITH MY HEART **I & II**

By **Linnea**

BOSS'N UP **I & II**

By **Royal Nicole**

I LOVE YOU TO DEATH

By Destiny J

I RIDE FOR MY HITTA

I STILL RIDE FOR MY HITTA

By **Misty Holt**

LOVE & CHASIN' PAPER

By **Qay Crockett**

TO DIE IN VAIN

By **ASAD**

BOOKS BY LDP'S CEO, CA$H

(CLICK TO PURCHASE)

TRUST IN NO MAN

TRUST IN NO MAN 2

TRUST IN NO MAN 3

BONDED BY BLOOD

SHORTY GOT A THUG

THUGS CRY

THUGS CRY 2

TRUST NO BITCH

TRUST NO BITCH 2

TRUST NO BITCH 3

TIL MY CASKET DROPS

RESTRAINING ORDER

RESTRAINING ORDER 2

IN LOVE WITH A CONVICT

Coming Soon

THUGS CRY 3

BONDED BY BLOOD 2

BOW DOWN TO MY GANGSTA

Printed in the USA
CPSIA information can be obtained
at www.ICGtesting.com
CBHW031207051223
2383CB00003B/72

9 781948 878388